To Jolene
From Kenny

LOST GIRL MISSING

JANET L. DE CASTRO

JL DE CASTRO

PO Box 25
Hummels Wharf, PA 17831-0025

Hard Cover: 978-1-7324219-1-2
Paperback: 978-1-7324219-0-5
Ebook: 978-1-7324219-2-9
Library of Congress Control Number: 2018907417
Copyright information available upon request - v. 1.0

Cover Design: Mark Saloff Designs / iStockphoto.com/Broccoli
Rope Graphic: Dreamstime.com / Gpgroup
Interior Design: J. L. Saloff

This novel is a work of fiction. All characters are the product of the author's imagination and are used fictitiously. Any resemblance between characters and real people, living or dead, is coincidental. Places and incidents are either fictitious, or are cited fictitiously. The story cites some real events, facts and places to support the plot, but the story is fiction and any resemblance to actual events is coincidental.

First Edition, 2018
Printed on acid free paper in the United States of America.

In loving memory of
Howard Sayre De Castro and Edith Liese De Castro
With eyes and mind wide open, anything is possible

Author's Note

I have altered natural features in Massachusetts for the story to flow. The settings are also more rural and devoid of towns and highways. The story has a blend of real and fictitious locations. All are used fictitiously.

"A woman is like a tea bag, you can't tell how strong she is until you put her in hot water." – *Eleanor Roosevelt*

The Foaling

Danuba snorted at hearing the weathervanes spinning like mad on the cupolas. The squeak of metal-on-metal and cold wind blowing through the loose barn boards was unbearable. Daylight was still several hours away, as her people timed it. The big red barn at Quimby Farm in Fairfield, Massachusetts was her shelter, her home. She had to wonder how safe she and her unborn foal were.

Her stable mates snorted and paced in their stalls. The barn boards moaned and creaked, ready to rip from the ribs of the building. Could the barn feel pain as her contractions increased? Danuba was about to foal for the third mud season in a row. This time felt different. As with the dangerous winds and cold outside, this foal felt wild and unpredictable.

In the early morning hours Danuba's restlessness

and pain continued to escalate with the rhythm of the howling winds. Danuba watched the other barn animals grow restless. The cats prowled for mice and swatted at each other. The roosters crowed well before sunrise. The sheep moved in circles within their pen only to change direction and circle around the other way.

Danuba peered at her pasture mate Lileana who stood silently in her stall. She hugged along the partition wall and looked through the horizontal oak board slats not knowing what to say or do. Sensing Lileana's fear and uncertainty, Danuba explained what would happen, since Lileana had never foaled, and assured her that everything would be okay.

The time had come for the little one's entry into the world. Danuba lay down and gently dropped her newborn onto a plush mound of straw made ready the day before by her people, Rose Quimby and Fiona. The newborn foal took her first breathes of air and lay kicking in the straw while being gently cleaned and prepared to nurse. Steam rose off of the wet foal, a reminder of the deadly cold waiting to snatch the new life away. The little one was on her hooves and wobbling around as if on a ship in rough seas. She found Danuba's warm nipple and suckled for the life-sustaining milk.

A hush came over the animals in the barn. The pain of foaling had subsided as did the winds outside. The cats, chickens, and sheep were so tired from their stir-rings that they fell into a slumber. The roosters were too tired to crow, within an hour of the sun breaking the horizon. Danuba, exhausted and shaking with a chill, and the little one settled in together on the soft straw and fell into a contented deep sleep. Danuba knew that Liliana stood guard awaiting the arrival of the people who would show up this morning, as they did every morning for feeding time.

Predawn

"Fi-o-na! Fi-o-na! Rise and shine, sleepy head," yelled Fiona's mother, Rose, from the kitchen. Rose hoped Fiona would get up and ready herself for her morning barn chores and then off to school without too much delay. This was the daily routine for the past year since she came to live with them.

Fiona stirred from under her warm, flannel-covered down comforter. She had heard Rose and subsequently Emmeric downstairs in the old farmhouse. The smell of a hot country breakfast being prepared was almost enough to convince her to get out of bed. Her stomach growled to the smell of bacon sizzling and oatmeal simmering on the stove. Pancake batter would soon be spooned onto the frying pan and spread into those wonderful round shapes that bubbled along the edges and browned a golden color. Fiona's musings were soon interrupted by the sound of dogs, bounding up the stairs and heading her way.

The collies represented two generations, mother and daughter. Tess, a black and white collie, had had a litter of pups within days of Fiona's arrival at the farm. She had pleaded with Rose and Emmeric to keep a couple of the pups. Rose had no problem with this and Emmeric relented, allowing one to stay as an additional working dog for the farm. The remaining pups were sold to other farmers in need of herding dogs.

The collies had made it to the top of the stairs now, running down the hall only moments from entering Fiona's room. Fiona pulled the comforter over her head. *No, not today, I really want to stay in bed, it's so miserable outside.*

She knew what to expect. It was the same scene every day, since she'd come to live with the Quimbys. But she really didn't want to get out of bed today. Gusts of wind pushed against the windows and she felt a draft from the electrical outlets along the outside wall of her bedroom. After all, the farmhouse was over one hundred years old and was never properly insulated.

Like clockwork, Tess and Tilda bolted into the bedroom. They barked in unison. Fiona screamed half with glee and half with anticipation of feeling the cold air once she left the warmth of her bed. Young Tilda smiled and wagged her tail. She jumped up on the bed and proceeded to squirm her way under the covers that were pulled up over Fiona's head. Tess, from the foot of the bed, grabbed a hold of the comforter with her teeth and pulled the covers off of Fiona in one fell swoop.

Tilda licked Fiona's face while Tess nibbled at her toes. Fiona slipped off of the bed and made her way down the long hallway to the bathroom. Tess had hold of one pajama leg, while Tilda tried nibbling at her feet and heels. She made it to the bathroom in one piece and looked in the mirror. Her red shoulder length hair was a mess. She grabbed a washcloth and gave a quick wash-up to her peaches and cream complexion accompanied by freckles over the bridge of her nose and across her upper cheeks. She brushed her teeth and pulled her hair into a band. Fiona's puffy eyes stared back at her from the reflection in the mirror. She hated getting up in the morning.

The tug-of-war walk back to the bedroom continued. Today was a thermal underwear day. She pulled a turtleneck on over her head. Then warm canvas pants and wool socks, appropriate for the work in the barn awaiting her arrival. She'd shower and change into school clothes after breakfast and chores.

The dogs escorted her along the hallway and down

the stairs. Tess was in the lead and Tilda behind to ensure that Fiona couldn't escape back to the warmth of bed.

Rose gave a stir to the oatmeal and shifted some of the bacon in the pan. In another five minutes she would begin the pancakes. She grabbed a mug of coffee and joined Emmeric at the kitchen table for a relaxing few sips. Rose smiled to herself knowing the dogs had done their job.

Rose, filled plates in hand, served Emmeric and Fiona and then herself. Everything smelled delicious, and tasted just as good. The Quimbys ate in relative silence. Tess and Tilda settled down at the feet of Emmeric and Fiona.

About ten minutes into the meal, Emmeric commented, as he did every morning to Fiona, "You're impossible. How can I properly run a farm around here when getting you up and moving is like moving a mountain? This is our livelihood. I depend on you."

Rose knew by looking at Fiona that she wished she was back in bed, where it was dark, and safe, and warm.

Rose reminded Emmeric, "She's been through more than enough for one lifetime, let alone for a thirteen-year-old girl."

Emmeric dialed back his mood to simmer and gently relayed to Rose and Fiona that since Danuba was within a week of her foaling date, at some point today the wood shavings used for bedding should be replaced by straw.

Rose held her coffee cup midway to her mouth while Fiona held a forkful of pancake and was about to put it in her mouth. Rose gave Emmeric a wide grin saying, "Yes, dear."

Fiona, almost in tears, choked down a piece of pancake. Even when she did something right, he never noticed or gave her credit. *Face it, if I was a boy he'd probably feel differently.*

Emmeric gave up his attempt at delegation of the day's work orders and went back to eating his breakfast in silent contemplation. He was outnumbered by women anyway.

"Rose, can I ask you about a really weird dream I had last night?" Fiona asked.

"Sure, honey."

"There was this horse-fish-thing that came out of a lake and was going to get me and I sunk in the mud and couldn't move. And Tess and Tilda appeared and barked. But then they had fangs and turned into wolves."

Emmeric squirmed in his chair and put his fork down. "What in God's name are you reading now?"

Rose shot Emmeric a look, then turned to Fiona. "Are you studying Celtic mythology in English class? The horse-fish-thing sounds like a Kelpie. As for Tess and Tilda, there's a connection between dogs and wolves…"

"Enough, of the Loch Ness Monster and werewolves." Emmeric stood up from the table. "The trash kids read today. We have work to do."

Fiona scowled at Emmeric. "Then the horse-fish turned into a boy with long red hair and went back into the lake. He wouldn't help me get unstuck from the mud."

Rose's face turned red and she and Emmeric looked at each other. "Did you see his face?" Rose asked.

"No."

Rose trembled and looked at her plate. "Do you remember anything else about the boy?"

"He wouldn't talk to me. Why? What does the dream mean?"

Rose got up from the table and rushed over to the sink, turning the water on and washed dishes.

Day One

Fiona's thoughts traveled far and wide this morning, especially after seeing Rose and Emmeric's reactions to her dream. She racked her brain trying to remember anything she could about her past. Now thirteen, Fiona began to grow out of her initial shyness after the first year of living with her new parents, but not her awkwardness. School was okay, and she had a small circle of friends, mostly other girls who lived on farms. Rose took Fiona to 4-H and Girl Scout meetings to encourage friendships and experiences, but the distance between farms and friends was like a great divide. Fiona felt isolated most of the time, but it wasn't Rose and Emmeric's fault.

Quimby Farm was located north-west of Deerfield, in Fairfield, western Massachusetts. This is where the adoption agency sent her to permanently live after her recovery, of two months of recuperation, rehabilitation and therapy at Mass General Hospital in Boston. The social worker explained the circumstances to Fiona numerous times, including the fact that her last name was Higgins (Fiona could not remember this). Her family had moved to a new town along the coast, Agawam Point, north of Boston. An all-consuming fire broke out, killing the rest of her family. Only Fiona survived. She suffered broken bones and a coma, resulting in amnesia and blocked memories due to trauma. She did not remember the fire or her escape. She had brief flashes of people, places and emotions, but wasn't sure that this was her family that she saw or felt, since no photos, or personal effects survived in the charred debris. The social worker told Fiona that investigators were unable to locate a living relative. The childless Quimbys adopted her, even though Emmeric felt awkward about having a young girl on the farm.

Fiona figured, *Life could be worse I suppose...but I wouldn't know.*

Breakfast was over. Rose stood over the sink. Emmeric pushed his chair in.

"Earth to Fiona. Snap out of your day dreaming," Emmeric said. "You're burning daylight. Get your coat and hat on. Get going!"

Fiona knew this part of the routine well. *But burning*

daylight, as Emmeric liked to say. How can I be burning daylight when it's still dark out? Tess and Tilda leaped from their spots under the table hearing the cue from Emmeric as, *time for the barn and wreaking havoc among the cats.*

In a swirl of moving bodies the four pushed out the back door and moved swiftly in the raw weather towards the barn, Fiona and the dogs in the lead. Immediately upon entering the barn, Tess and Tilda barked. Emmeric showed a more purposeful stride. A tingle, like an electric charge, raced up and down her spine. She'd never felt it before. She ran to Danuba's stall and gasped, mouth wide open. There were two horses in the stall. A small almost white horse with big brown eyes. It stood beside golden Danuba. It's ears barely reached to the top of the stall door.

"Emmeric!"

Emmeric raced to Fiona's side and smiled, saying, "Happy birthday, little one. You picked one heck of a morning to arrive. Fiona, get Rose on the intercom. Tell her to call the vet, we've got a new Haflinger foal. The dishes can wait."

"Can I go inside the stall and see her? Or maybe it's a him?"

"It's a her. I can tell already," Emmeric said softly, his head cocked sideways. "Go in quietly and slowly.

Danuba won't mind as long as you don't scare the foal. Crouch into a smaller profile. Let her come and smell you."

Fiona was in awe of the newborn foal. "She is so cute."

Her coat, an off-white color, thick and curly, nothing like the heavy textured, golden color of Danuba. The foal moved slowly on skinny wobbly legs toward Fiona and sniffed her hand, then turned back to the safety of Danuba to suckle. Fiona thought, *Safety and food seems to be what all animals desire. It's universal.*

Rose arrived at the barn in time to see the foal suckle. "I see she's made friends with Fiona. Oh, Emmeric, she is precious. She looks perfect."

Emmeric said, "We'll see what the vet says after he completes his exam. Did the answering service tell you who's on call?"

"Yes," Rose said, "Doctor McKenna."

Hearing Emmeric and Rose, Fiona's only thought revolved around getting out of school today.

"And by the way," Rose said, "you don't have to go to school, this one time."

Fiona came out of the stall. She was thrilled and spun around in a circle. "Can I name her?" She had a list of boy and girl names a mile long in her head. She constantly doodled name combinations on her notebook in school despite looks of reproach from her teachers.

Emmeric had explained the naming system for the Haflinger breed. A colt's name must begin with the same first letter as the sire's name, whereas a filly's name must begin with the same first letter as the dam's name.

Fiona slowly walked back into Danuba's stall. The foal approached Fiona and sniffed her hand again. Looking at the foal, quietly Fiona said, "Okay, little one, what are we going to name you? In my dreams, a name kept coming to me, but it doesn't start with a D."

Fiona turned to Emmeric and Rose, "Please, Emmeric, can I give her a barn name instead? A nickname?"

"How do you know about barn names? I'm impressed."

"We learned about them in 4-H. You know, Emmeric, Haflingers make great driving-show horses too, not just work horses. I bet she'd be a good project horse for me. I could train her." She sidled over to Danuba and the foal and brushed its curly short mane with her hand. "Think of all the ribbons we could win, girl. You and me and a fancy cart. All dressed up: you in beautiful harness, me in a beautiful outfit and fancy hat…"

"Slow down, Fiona! A barn name, remember. Rose and I will come up with her registered name for her papers… She'll be leaving us in about five months, after she's weaned. Don't get attached! She's for sale and that's the end of it!"

Fiona leaned on the stall door, head resting on hands, the G word swimming around in her brain. The foal sniffed and grabbed Fiona's coat.

"Hey, Girl! That's it, G…Gilly Girl."

Gilly cocked her head at Fiona. Danuba gave a soft whinny in what sounded like approval. Fiona smiled at the new horse family. It would be harder to convince Emmeric and Rose to keep a foal.

"I wish I had a smartphone so that I could take newborn pictures to send to my friends. It isn't fair…I'm the only one—"

"We've been all through this Fiona, I work…" Emmeric looked at Rose. "We work hard enough for what we have. The animals are our livelihood. You can't keep them all. Be thankful that you have a computer. You ranted and raved…"

Rose touched his arm to quiet him.

Fiona felt her face flush and turned to leave. "I'll feed the others."

"Dear, grab my old camera out of the hallway dresser," Rose said. "It should still have film in it."

spring

Spring arrived in the West Deerfield River Valley. Forsythia pushed out yellow flowers on shrubbery, high and dry of the remnant brown-gray muck and mire patches. Purple and white crocuses had bloomed during mud season, and small yellow and white narcissus provided at least a glimmer of the new season. The pastures started to green, and the days grew longer.

Lambing season began in earnest, and additional foals were born to other mares from other breeds of horses. But Fiona's heart remained with the gentle Haflinger breed and especially the new foal Gilly. Chicks hatched-out in the hatchery. Spring proved an incredibly busy season for the Quimbys, and Fiona lent a hand in all manner of farm chores when she was home from school. The extra work forced her to stop going to 4-H and Girl Scout meetings. She didn't mind. Hanging out in the barn made her feel special. The horses nudged her, and nickered, and whinnied which was their horse talk to her. She loved the physical nature of the farm work and getting her hands dirty. And, most of all, she got to spend lots of time with Gilly. It felt like she'd done this her whole life. And she knew she was in-touch with the animals. She sensed when they weren't feeling well and when they wanted to be brushed or needed extra water. She felt loved and wanted. It was as if they could read each other's thoughts.

One sunny April morning, when Gilly was four weeks old, Fiona and Emmeric were out riding the fence lines on the UTV and checking the pastures for groundhog holes and rocks. Emmeric jumped out of the vehicle, grabbed a shovel out of the back and filled in a series of holes. Fiona wore heavy duty suede gloves. She slid out of her seat and pulled at the large rocks which had sprouted after winter's thaw. She carried them back to the vehicle. "I should have brought the wheelbarrow."

"Grab the spackle pail for now. Don't let it get too heavy," Emmeric said.

"What's with the saw horse and cans?" Fiona asked.

Emmeric smiled, a gleam in his eyes, "For later."

Hours later, hot and tired, they finished one pasture.

The back of the UTV was laden with rocks, the shovel on top. The cans were inside a pail, sawhorse against the rocks. They sat under a tree with fresh young buds, swigging down cold drinks that Rose had packed for them and wolfing down peanut butter sandwiches.

"What's the surprise?" Fiona asked.

Emmeric opened the glove box and pulled out a pink metal slingshot. It glistened in the sunlight that punctured through the tree branches.

"Awesome!"

"Do you really like it?" Emmeric handed the cool metal device over to her waiting hands.

"I do. Really. I don't think I've ever had one."

"Good, let's practice." Emmeric set up the saw horse and cans. "Let's try twenty-five feet."

"Hold it like this. Pull back, arms held such." He positioned her. "Release. Good." Emmeric pulled a box of metal pellets from his pocket. "Now with a pellet. Aim. Release."

Plink.

"Great first shot," Emmeric said.

"Do you think so?" Fiona said coyly.

"Probably beginners luck. Well, let's see. You've got four more cans."

Plink. Plink. Plink. Plink.

Fiona fell on the ground, laughing.

Emmeric's face turned red with embarrassment. "Hey, wait. Not fair. What aren't you telling me?"

If you'd take an interest in what I do in school or scouting you'd know... She kept her anger in check. "I'm the top archery girl in my class!"

"Oh, you sure you never went hunting or anything?"

Yup, there's the sarcastic Emmeric I know. "Not that I can remember." She took in a deep breath and blew air out to calm herself. "Why are you teaching me to use a slingshot?"

"The groundhogs are one reason. Varmints in general. If you see any, you need to kill them."

"Me? Kill something?" Goosebumps appeared on Fiona's arms and she shuddered.

"If one of your *precious* horses falls in a groundhog hole, it'll break a leg and I'll be out a sale. Weasels and fox can kill off the whole chicken house in a night, and the sheep...Need me to go on? This is serious business."

"Got it. Mind if we stop for today? I'm beat." Fiona slipped the slingshot into her shirt pocket and picked up the cans.

"Here, don't forget to keep ammo with you." Emmeric carried the sawhorse. "Moving targets next time – should be more of a challenge." He gloated.

♥

Gilly's long legs grew stronger by the day, and so did her curiosity about everything. Despite Danuba and Lileana's efforts to teach her about the dangers "out there" and awareness skills, she managed accidents and mishaps regularly.

Gilly, head lowered, listened to another round of lectures. "Just last week you managed to fall into the deep drainage ditch that I have repeatedly shown you, on the edge of the pasture," warned Danuba. "It is out of bounds! What were you thinking?"

Gilly had recovered from the harrowing fall and subsequent rescue by the people and the local fire department. Specialized lift equipment had been brought in to hoist her out of the ditch.

Dr. McKenna came when Gilly was brought back to the barn and proclaimed, "It was a miracle she didn't break any bones, just some cuts and abrasions that will heal up," but could not guarantee whether or not there would be any permanent scars.

Gilly had lowered her head in response to Emmeric's displeasure, feeling guilty for the way he was talking to Rose and Fiona. "I don't know if I can get my asking price if she's scarred and battered. She's too headstrong. I can't wait for this filly to be gone."

Not even a week later, from the near-disaster of the ditch, Gilly teetered on the brink of another mishap. She had managed to push her rump through the rails in the fence in an attempt to scratch said rump. She had heard the snap of a weak board. Before realizing what had happened, her body folded in half, and she lay on the ground. Hooves pointed up in the air. She was in such an awkward position that she couldn't get up. Danuba and Lileana had no luck dislodging her either. Lileana grabbed the broken rail pushing and pulling. Danuba and Lileana whinnied and snorted like crazy, trying to get the attention of Emmeric or Fiona in the sheep pasture. They galloped around until they caught someone's eye. Then they galloped back over to where Gilly lay in a panic on the ground. Danuba attempted to settle Gilly, to keep her from hurting herself.

Gilly watched as Emmeric and Fiona hopped on the UTV, started it up, and sped along to the horse pasture. Fiona jumped out before Emmeric came to a complete halt. She ran to Gilly and knelt down beside her on the outside of the pasture.

Fiona said very softly, "I'm here now, girl, everything's going to be okay." Gilly felt some of the panic subside. There was a special tone in her person's voice that soothed her. Fiona stroked Gilly's curly flaxen mane and white blaze, now showing two prominent freckles the color of her slightly darkening body. Fiona's warm touch sent a soothing vibration through her nerves.

"You've got freckles just like me." Fiona hadn't noticed them before since Gilly's coat was so light in color. Gilly smiled to herself and softened her eyes at Fiona.

Danuba and Lileana had calmed down. They watched over the scene at a gentle pace back and forth.

Emmeric grabbed a lead rope from the back of the UTV and threw it to Fiona. She snapped it onto Gilly's pink halter. Fiona held tight to the rope. Emmeric gently moved her legs sideways, permitting gravity to take over. Gilly's legs fell to the outside of the pasture. She gathered up her strength and pushed her body weight onto her long awkward legs. Gilly knew she was in trouble from the disappointed looks on everyone. She'd especially let Fiona down.

"Fiona, walk Gilly around a bit so I can check her out for injuries. As soon as she's weaned, she's out of here," growled Emmeric.

Fiona's face turned beet red. *If I make a mistake will he get rid of me the way he is with Gilly?* She was angry with Emmeric. Fiona whispered out of his hearing range, "Gilly, I need to come up with a plan, and fast. If Emmeric had his way, you'd be gone tomorrow. I won't let that happen."

Gilly gave a soft nicker, nodding her head as if in agreement, then rubbed her face along Fiona's and planted a wet lick on her mouth.

Run-In Shed

"Fiona, how's it going with Gilly today?" Emmeric asked. "I've got some folks coming over from Warwick to take a look at her, around three o'clock. What can we show them?"

Fiona felt a flush creep up her neck toward her face and turned away so he couldn't see her mounting displeasure. The summer sunlight added more warmth to the flush of her skin. She worked Gilly in the round pen on a lunge line. Gilly had progressed in her basic training to the point of advanced moves. Fiona wouldn't show this to Emmeric or any strangers. She took in a deep breath and cued Gilly with the line and whip and a cluck of the tongue. Gilly circled clockwise, at the walk, then halted on command. She reversed direction and repeated the routine. Gilly walked forward toward Fiona and then backed away from her as commanded.

Gilly stood still when Fiona dropped the line in a coil on the ground. Now each leg was picked up one by one with a gentle tap as a prompt and placed down. Gilly remained standing, hardly fidgeting. Fiona petted her saying, "Good job, girl."

"I can't believe what you've done in such a short time with her. This will really help today in showing her off to the prospective buyers."

Fiona cringed and quietly watched as Emmeric turned, smile intact, and headed to the poultry area of the barn.

His praise was like a double-edged sword. She appreciated it, and it made her feel important. But, the more she trained Gilly, the better the chances were that she could be sold sooner rather than later.

She led Gilly back to pasture to be with Danuba and Lileana. The two horses came forward to greet them at the gate.

"Gilly, I know I'm not supposed to get attached to you. I don't want you to go. I love you." Fiona gave Gilly a gentle brushing and hug, and in thanks received a nicker and a warm wet kiss before turning her out with the others.

Fiona swore she heard Gilly say, "I feel the same too." She turned around to listen again. Just to be sure.

Before three, Fiona heard a truck rumble onto the

gravel driveway. She yelled to Emmeric that the people from Warwick had arrived. She ran out to the pasture to round up Gilly and clipped the lunge line to the halter, and walked her to the round pen where they would run through the exercises. Emmeric introduced Mr. and Mrs. "Whatever" from Warwick to Fiona – but she paid no real attention to them. *No way are they going to take Gilly from me.*

Fiona cued Gilly as before, and they ran through the routine. She could hear the oohs! and ahhs! coming from Mr. and Mrs. "Whatever" as Emmeric talked up the virtues of owning such a fine filly.

I need a plan.

Mr. and Mrs. thanked Emmeric and Fiona. "We're very impressed with Gilly and will get back to you in a few days with our decision. Young lady, you've done a fine job."

Fiona was devastated.

I need a plan.

At three months old, Gilly still shared a stall with Danuba. Late afternoon in the barn, Danuba looked on while Fiona gave Gilly a good brushing and knew she would have to give "the talk" to Gilly tonight. Danuba said in a soft, sad voice to Lileana, "It's time for Gilly to know the truth. She will leave us soon to begin a new life on a farm with others."

Lileana lowered her head, looked through the stall slats at Danuba, and said, "I will miss her too."

Danuba softly nickered at Fiona and Gilly. The foal nodded her head. Fiona smiled at the attention Gilly was getting.

♡

Gilly sensed that this had been a long day of emotional ups and downs for Fiona. She had felt Fiona's tension all day. For the first time, the future felt uncertain. Gilly watched as Fiona came into the barn well before sunset. The long summer days had stretched daylight out to its full length as if on a taut canvas.

"Okay, girls, time to eat," Fiona said. Gilly perked her ears forward and greeted Fiona with pleasure. Fiona placed hay and oats in the stalls and poured water into buckets.

Emmeric and Rose tended the larger herd of mares and foals, brought into the barn for evening meal. This meant that Gilly could have Fiona almost all to herself.

Danuba was about to say something to Gilly. She sensed sadness in her Mother, but couldn't imagine why.

"Gilly, there will be a day not far from now that you will be leaving us."

"What do you mean?" Gilly said. A feeling of panic swelled in her belly.

"One day soon you will be sold and go to live on a farm with another family."

Gilly pawed the ground. "No! I'm not leaving you and Lileana and Fiona."

"You have no say in the matter," Danuba said. "This happened to me, and to my mother, and to all horses around. Our people sell us so we can pull plows or carts. This is our job with people."

Gilly threw her head back and reared up on hind legs, coming down hard. Then she bucked, spun around, and almost kicked Danuba. The next kick hit the water bucket. It came off the bracket and crashed to the ground. Water splashed the walls. The filly thrashed and emitted a cry of fear which caused the sheep to baa. The hens cackled and roosters crowed as if a fox was attacking. Tess and Tilda howled and chased the barn cats around, sending them crashing into each other in their haste to escape. Bedlam reigned.

Emmeric rushed over with a lead rope. He snapped it onto Danuba's halter, and led her out, and into Lileana's stall.

Lileana, panicked by the sudden violent outburst, raised her head and got wide eyed. She snorted to

Danuba. Danuba snorted back. Gilly sounded a trum-
peting alarm.

Emmeric yelled to Rose, "Grab a syringe and bottle
of sedative from the medicine cabinet."

♡

Fiona pressed her body to a wall opposite the stall, horrified. A crazed Haflinger had replaced her sweet Gilly.
She couldn't breathe. The sight of Gilly in a state of panic
was replaced by a vision.

*She was in her bedroom. A dark human-like shadow
towered in front of her. Flames licked up the walls behind
the shadow. She backed into a window, unable to escape
the shadow or the flames.*

The vision melted away as quickly as it had appeared.
She was holding her chest, staring at Gilly again. But she
couldn't breathe. Her head pounded. *What happened?
What was that?* Her hands were cold and shaking. She
willed herself to think instead about Gilly.

Rose arrived at Emmeric's side and prepared the
injection. Emmeric grabbed another lead rope to attach
to Gilly.

"Wait," Fiona shouted.

Emmeric said, "We don't have time for games."

"No, no it's not like that…" Now weak and still shaking from the vision Fiona stumbled over and grabbed

his arm and blocked him from entering the stall. She knew that Emmeric was furious with her for interfering.

"I need to sedate her. The foal is ill. Rose, do something with Fiona."

"Gilly's not sick, Emmeric. She—she's upset about something."

"How would you know?"

"I—I can sense it. It's the way she's crying out. She's scared. Let me go in and talk to her." Fiona inched her way to the stall door.

Fiona watched Gilly circle in the stall. She was no longer bucking and rearing up.

Rose held Emmeric's shoulder gently. "Let her try. Gilly's calmed down a lot."

"So help me…if you get hurt Fiona…" Emmeric said.

Fiona carefully entered the stall. Gilly stood quietly, head down. Slowly, Gilly approached, as Fiona whispered softly, "Girl I know you're upset. What can I do to help?" Fiona kissed her freckled blaze.

Rose said, "You have to admit it, she has a way with the foal."

Emmeric grunted, "Huh."

Fiona put her hand out for the lead rope. "Let me take her out for a walk."

"Careful. If she starts up again, get away from her."

"Will do. Come on, girl," said Fiona confidently.

She led Gilly out of the barn at a slow, somber walk. And figured they'd as soon keep walking. But today was not the right day for the "long, one-way, walk."

As they entered the pasture, the warm orange sun hung low in the sky. It would be dark soon. Tess and Tilda joined Fiona and Gilly. The dogs circled to keep them rounded up. Fiona swore that both dogs had smiles on their faces. Gilly threw her head up and down in a playful gesture. The temper tantrum appeared to be forgotten.

Fiona unsnapped the lead line from the foal's bright pink halter and allowed her to run free in the pasture with the dogs.

"Come on girls, let's head out to the run-in shed. This is new territory for you, Gilly." *Yeah, and I bet you've already snuck out there.* Fiona couldn't shake the scare of the vision from her head. Goosebumps ran up and down her arms. *Was any of it real?*

Fiona couldn't keep up with her four-footed friends. She could've on the UTV or at least kept everyone in view. They would have to return to the barn soon, it was getting late. The sun was an orange slice in the sky above the horizon.

♡

Gilly was first to reach the run-in shed, but now by herself she was afraid. The dogs arrived a few seconds later.

A strange voice emanated from the rafters of the little building. "Who's there? Who's there?"

Gilly turned and ran. She bolted from the building, almost running down Fiona.

"Whoa, Gilly Girl. What are you scared of?" Fiona said, out of breath.

Gilly circled back to where Fiona stood, and pushed up against her. Knocking her to the ground she snorted, pawed the ground an inch from Fiona's hand. In apology for knocking her down, Gilly licked Fiona's face. Gilly didn't realize her own strength. *How light Fiona is. Danuba and Lileana would have stood firm. I've got to get her up on her feet.* She nudged her head under Fiona's arm to help her off the ground. The dogs came to Fiona's aid as well, tugged at her shirt and nipped at her heel to get her to rise.

Wow, Gilly's strong. I've got to be more careful. She's no puppy dog. She's a strong, unpredictable horse. "Okay… let's see what all the fuss is about," Fiona said, wiping at her pants.

They trudged their way to the run-in. The animals heard the voice as, "Who's there? Who's there?"

"It's not a mountain lion or monster," Fiona said. "It's an owl saying hoot, hoot."

Gilly was not convinced that Fiona was right on this point. The creature talked again, directly to Gilly. The piercing golden eyes felt like sharp knives, slicing through her soul. She had never seen such a fierce creature. She wanted to run again but trusted that Fiona wouldn't let anything happen to her. And Tess and Tilda would snap at the creature if he tried anything.

"Who are you?" the owl asked.

Gilly whinnied shyly, "I'm Gilly and these are my friends Fiona, Tess, and Tilda." Gilly pointed to each with her muzzle.

Tess and Tilda barked a greeting.

Gilly whinnied, "Who are you?"

The owl puffed out his chest, "I'm Eldar, and this is my home!"

♡

Fiona smiled at the cacophony coming from among the animals and said, "Leave the owl alone. It's getting dark. Time to head back."

Fiona knew she was running out of time. Gilly's tantrum might mean that Emmeric would want to sell her even sooner. Later that night, Fiona pretended she was doing homework but she was really researching on the computer where to run away to. And the West Deerfield River was probably a good place to start. There was a forever rumor in school about an old fortress from the French-Indian Wars someplace deep in the north woods.

The Race

Sitting at the desk in her bedroom, Fiona pressed the ON button. The screen came to life as the computer loaded information onto the display. The desktop, a picture of wild mustangs from somewhere out west, greeted her next move on the keyboard. She typed in the website address which showed satellite images from just about anywhere on earth. Her first destination tonight, Agawam Point north of Boston, past Marble Head along the sea coast.

The vision she had had earlier bothered her so much that it left her with even more questions about her former life. She went to her closet and got down on hands and knees. She crawled all the way in and backed out, pulling a small wood box with her. Rose had given her the simple box with a rose carved in the top, made by Rose's father for her when she was Fiona's age. A "Memory

Box" Rose called it. Fiona opened the box and picked up the hospital bracelet: Fiona Higgins, Mass General Hospital. This was from her old life. She placed it back in the box. She retrieved and unfolded a piece of paper. The social worker at the hospital in Boston had given it to her. It contained her former address.

She sat back at her desk. "Argh, this computer is so slow, Tilda. Dial-up. Emmeric doesn't see the need for anything faster. He doesn't get it."

Tilda sat with her head on Fiona's lap and reacted to her comment with a tilt of the head. Google Earth finally came up, and Fiona wasted no time in typing in the address where her family perished: 1644 Quahog Drive, Agawam Point, Massachusetts. Nothing about this address seemed familiar. Slowly, very slowly, an image built up on the screen.

This was her first attempt at viewing where she used to live. She couldn't do it before today. She didn't have the courage. Having the vision pushed her to look. What she saw shocked her. A blackened pit in the ground, earth scorched all around. An updated image by Google Earth.

Her body and breathing stiffened. A vision replaced the blackness on the screen.

She was in her bedroom. A dark shadow came towards her, hands outstretched. A man? A boy? Flames licked up the walls behind the shadow. She was backed up to a window. No place to go. She felt a shove. Falling, falling...

Thump! Fiona found herself lying on the floor. Tilda stood over her, whimpering and licking her face. Fiona sat up and turned her head sideways so she wouldn't have to look at the computer screen. She reached up and turned the computer off.

Rose yelled from downstairs, "Fiona what's going on up there?"

"Some books fell."

"Are you alright? It sounded heavier than *some* books."

"I'm okay. I'm going to bed now."

"Okay. See you in the morning," Rose said.

Research would have to wait.

An August scorcher today. At seven in the morning the heat and humidity had already set in. Fiona would have to work five-month-old Gilly early and keep her in the cool barn at mid-day with the rest of the horses.

Fiona readied herself for the day, helped by the dogs. She splashed water on her face and pulled her hair into a ponytail. After chores and Gilly's training session, a shower and sundress would feel great. She ran down the stairs, successfully avoiding the dogs along the way.

"What's the rush this morning?" Rose said, while

placing boxes of cereal on the kitchen table along with blueberries from the bushes in the garden.

"I want to get out to the barn and feed the girls early. It's gonna be hot and I won't be able to work with Gilly much."

"Hasn't she been trained enough? The lovely couple from Warwick should be picking her up in a few weeks."

An angry flush crept up Fiona's face. "I didn't know that Gilly was already sold. Emmeric never said anything back in June! I figured she was still mine." Fiona was on the verge of tears.

Rose said tenderly, "I'm sorry we didn't tell you sooner, sweetie. We knew you'd be upset. We explained all this to you in the beginning." The words stumbled from her lips. "We were trying to wait as long as possible."

"Where's Emmeric?" asked Fiona, now wiping her eyes.

Rose's cheeks turned pink. "He's fixing a few loose fence boards in the sheep pasture. And I think he mentioned there are some additional loose boards out at the run-in shed."

"I hadn't noticed any bad boards out there." Fiona hated lying to Rose. She felt as though Rose and Emmeric had deceived her about Gilly.

Maybe he'll be too busy to get to the run-in. Gilly might be able to fit through the turnstile gate. If she could line the spokes up just so, and Gilly wouldn't panic from the confinement...

Her plan was shaping up even though the point of egress presented a fly in the ointment. But she'd have to try anyway. Gilly was so big now. She figured with the girth tape that the foal weighed about five-hundred pounds compared to her own one-hundred.

"I'll be back for breakfast after I feed everyone. I'm taking the dogs with me."

Tails wagged, and they headed to the back door in the mud room.

"Okay then," Rose said.

Fiona watched as Rose sat down with a cup of coffee, shoulders slumped. It looked like she had the weight of the world on her shoulders. *I hope it wasn't from me.*

The morning training session went really well. Gilly could hold increased weight on her back, which could be dangerous for the filly at such a young age. But the training was gradual, over many weeks. Now to test the next step. Fiona stood on a tree trunk, gently swung her leg up and over, and sat on Gilly for a few minutes. She patted her neck. "Good girl. You're the best."

Gilly swung her head up and down. Fiona slid off of five-month-old Gilly who was definitely not old enough to ride. Fiona wanted to get her used to everything she could think of, not knowing what they might encounter on the journey. They finished

along the back pasture. Fiona w

with books. They both needed s

The sun had reached its pir

was time to quit. Fiona hosed Gilly on and raked the

water from her coat before returning her to the barn

and Danuba, who by now was ready for Gilly to suckle,

even though she was not producing as much milk. Gilly

ate oats and hay and grazed in pasture like the adults.

Fiona's deadline was closing in, and the stress was kill-

ing her. She'd chewed her fingernails down to nothing.

Good thing she never wore nail polish.

Got to go!

The old farmhouse was very warm. Rose kept the

shades drawn on the south and west sides, keeping the

bright sunlight out. Ceiling fans hummed a slow tune

and kept the air moving.

Fiona trudged upstairs with her backpack to her

room, dogs on her heals. She pulled the chain on her

fan, plopped the bag on the floor, and sat at the desk. She

turned the computer on. The screen came to life. Fiona

showered and changed quickly in order to get back to

the waiting computer.

She wouldn't type in Agawam Point. The keys she

tapped spelled out Fairfield, Massachusetts. She plopped

back in her chair to wait for the image to build on the

en. Once done, she zoomed out to view a larger image of the West Deerfield River Valley on Google Earth.

The terrain of the River Valley resembled a patchwork quilt. A bumpy one, with massive farm fields; green, brown and gold bordered by hedgerows and trees; hills and ridges; erosion contoured gullies; and blue spider vein creeks and streams, including the arterial West Deerfield River itself.

Fiona and Gilly would have to travel north and west following along the river. This side of the river had hiking trails and farm after farm. But at some point they would have to be on the other side of the river. The Mohawk Trail side. A girl and her horse on a "hike" might arouse suspicion. They could cross the foot bridge at Craggy Frog Bottoms. She had learned about the crossing at Girl Scouts. Her Cadet group was scheduled to go on an encampment with another troop. The footbridge was considered a tricky crossing since it swings with the weight of hikers on it and high waters cover the bridge, especially after heavy rains.

The bridge finally came into view on the satellite image.

Good.

Kids in school loved spreading rumors about haunted places, even about the old fort from the Indian

Wars. Fiona never heard adults talk about it, and no way could she ask Rose or Emmeric. They'd become suspicious. Fiona Googled "Forts, French-Indian Wars, Massachusetts, Vermont." No luck. A couple of hits on the legend of an old fort along the Green River. She went back to the satellite image.

"Great, the West Deerfield merges with the Green River." She said aloud.

Back to the other screen, and a story that a hiker named Claire Ward had written some thirty-odd-years ago. This was debunked by historical experts and archeologists who never spotted any fort remains. The woman had no proof and could not lead others back to a fort.

Even if this fort doesn't really exist I'm bound to find an abandoned hunting cabin or farm. Any desolate area where no one could find them. She'd hunt for food, even though the thought of killing animals made her sick. She had learned about berries and nuts – what was edible in survival training. She planned to bring water and snacks for the trip. Mostly granola, protein bars and dried fruit from the pantry. She didn't know how much to pack. This was the tricky part. Gilly could graze and drink water along the way. No problem. The dogs would have to come too. A bit of a complication. She didn't mean to take the dogs. They'd end up following her despite being told to stay in the barn. The dogs' meals would be more difficult. She needed to pack bags of kibble. The fort or at least an abandoned shelter had to be somewhere. She didn't want to lose Gilly. *Stop daydreaming.* She scrolled up. *Very desolate. Just woods. I wonder if this is Vermont.* The image further north refused to come up on the screen. She scrolled down a couple of times. Farm fields and water. The picture was good. Scrolled up two times, no way, nothing. She slumped back in her chair rolling her head back. The fort is supposed to be between the Monroe area and Vermont.

"We just have to go for it," she declared to Tess and Tilda.

The dogs stared at Fiona and studied her as she talked. Her next problem was when? The only time she'd be alone at the farm was for two hours on Sunday. They took turns going to church because someone had to mind the animals. This Sunday was her turn to stay behind. That would give her a two hour head start.

My last day of farm chores!

Fiona got up from her chair and plopped spread-eagle on the bed. The ceiling fan spun. A slow whir sound filled her ears. "One, two, three. One, two, three, fo-ur." She studied the blades. "Four not three." Her stomach flipped. She closed her eyes. "Something's missing. It's not right. Someone else was in the house. Mom, Dad, me and…"

Eldar

Fiona climbed the ladder to the hayloft for one last check that everything was packed and hidden away. One thing she better put in the backpack, just in case – the pink metal slingshot. It was pretty and cool to the touch, and a box of pellets. But she knew she could never use it, really. Maybe threaten something away with it. Shoot nearby to scare an animal away. Kill something, never. School would begin in a couple of weeks, but Fiona and her backpack would not be there.

She didn't think she could have ever have liked first days of school. It made her nervous now. All of a sudden, old pictures in her mind of new dresses and the high step up on to the yellow school bus flooded her head. *Was this a memory?* The smell of a woman's freshly shampooed hair, mint and lemon, and the encouraging push up the steps given by a soft hand. Her mother!

She just had a real memory. Not one of those horrible visions. She cried with joy in the hayloft over this recaptured flash to her past. *It's coming back...*

♥

The Day had finally arrived.

Fiona awoke to her noisy alarm clock at 5:30 A.M. *Oh, I hate early mornings. But no choice today – all the chores have to be done before we go, even Emmeric's. Bad enough I'm stealing their animals.* Emmeric and Rose were serving as ushers at church and would leave a half hour earlier than normal. Fiona planned on going as soon as possible, to get a head start in case a search party was sent to look for her and the missing filly and dogs.

I can't leave Tess and Tilda behind. The dogs complicate things. Emmeric and Rose are going to hate me. Besides, the girls will keep us safe.

It was a warm day, but doable for traveling. Butterflies fluttered in her stomach. The thought of eating breakfast with Emmeric and Rose without getting sick was making her sick. She peeked on her desk to make sure the note she left was still there.

Where else would it be? Come on, girl, get a grip.

She opened it up and re-read it. In the note she apologized for taking the filly and dogs and thanked them for adopting her, "With fondness, Fiona," not knowing how to leave it off. It wasn't "love." *I don't feel like I belong here. I'm temporary like Gilly, and when they've had enough of me, I'll find myself with another family.*

Fiona managed to feed the animals while Emmeric and Rose readied themselves for church. She wiped her sweaty brow with the back of a gloved hand. She completed her chores in record time. She'd collect eggs and do Emmeric's work after breakfast, just before desertion.

Rose looked up at the sound of the screen door slamming in the mud room and click of the dogs' nails on the linoleum floor. Tilda barked impatiently to be fed.

"The dogs are excited this morning, Emmeric," Rose said.

"No wonder, Fiona rushed through the barn feedings. She's got the dogs all worked up. What's up with her today?" Emmeric asked before taking a sip of coffee.

Fiona came into the kitchen and poured a glass of orange juice. Her face was red and wet with sweat.

"What's the hurry? You may as well come to church with us," Rose said.

Fiona almost choked on her juice. "No, no…I've still got Emmeric's work ahead of me."

"Don't take any short cuts. Spend the time you need and get the job done right," Emmeric said suspiciously.

Rose heard panic in Fiona's voice. "Are you okay?" She felt her head for fever.

"The heat's got me a bit. I think I rushed too much."

"Why?" Rose asked.

"I wanted to have breakfast with you and Emmeric. I'll slow down after I eat, and you've left for church."

"You don't want to get sick, do you?"

"No, that's the last thing I want." Fiona walked over and gave Rose and Emmeric each a peck on the cheek.

Rose and Emmeric traded a curious look.

Emmeric and Rose drove away. Dust rose from the gravel where the tires passed. Fiona waved good-bye.

Alone at last to finish up. I still have to collect the eggs and get the sheep out. Remember to put the note on the kitchen table.

More butterflies must have hatched in her stomach. She grabbed her belly, bending slightly. "My stomach," she moaned to Tess and Tilda, as the butterflies circled around her breakfast.

She retrieved her backpack and duffle from the hayloft. The horses looked at her expectantly, ears forward, ready to go out to pasture. Danuba and Lileana whinnied softly in anticipation of the stall doors opening. The trick was to keep Gilly in while Danuba was released. *Okay, that worked.* Danuba looked back to see Gilly still in the stall. Gilly paced and whinnied in her high pitch. Fiona grabbed a whip off the wall and tapped Danuba and Lileana to keep a forward momentum. Danuba looked back again but moved out of the barn. As if she knew what today was. The start of the weaning.

Fiona re-entered the barn and Gilly's stall with halter and lead rope in hand. She did remember to pack another halter, a size bigger, and lead rope for emergencies. Fiona took a calming breath. If Gilly sensed she was nervous, it would make her nervous as well.

Keep breathing. Act like this is a regular training day.

Fiona haltered Gilly and attached the duffle bag as they had practiced. The backpack she had already swung onto her own back. "Come on, girl, walk easy."

The four made their way to the farthest pasture and the run-in shed. Tess and Tilda ran ahead of Fiona and Gilly. "So far, so good," Fiona said out loud. "I hope that pesky owl isn't there." The run-in was in sight. The dogs stood inside the run-in, looking up and barking.

Fiona jumped nervously and tugged too hard on the lead attached to Gilly. It was no mystery what the dogs were barking at. She composed herself, and then spoke softly to her foal. "Gilly, stay calm when we get inside. We won't be there long, and then we'll go through the turnstile. It's just an *owl*. It can't hurt you."

Gilly bobbed her head up and down.

The next thing Fiona heard along with the bark of the dogs made her wish she had gone to church today. She looked up in the rafters.

"Why must you wake me? Why must you wake me?" said the shrill voice.

A chill ran down her spine. "No way! I'm not hearing this. Owls can't talk!"

The owl rotated his head toward Fiona and Gilly and looked at them with piercing golden eyes. "Don't listen. Don't listen."

Fiona's heart pounded. She held tight to Gilly's lead so she wouldn't bolt. "How come I can understand you now and I couldn't before?"

"You heard, but you did not listen." the owl replied. "You are standing in a doorway to greater understanding. But with understanding comes danger."

"Well, owl, you're a rude bird."

"No, I'm Eldar."

"I wasn't expecting an answer. You're probably a vision like the shadow."

Eldar's head swiveled. "I can assure you, girl, I am very real."

"I'm Fiona." *I can't believe I'm having this conversation. Someone wake me.*

Fiona tried to relax. But was ready to run for the hills.

"Why are you traveling today?" Eldar asked.

Fiona bit her lip. "We're just out for a walk. That's all."

"I've watched and listened for months. I tried to introduce myself to her the day she knocked you down."

"Thanks," Fiona said sarcastically.

The owl's head swiveled. "That is nothing compared to what's ahead of you should you go through the run-in to the other side. Fiona, girl, you are not ready for what awaits you. Now is not the time."

A chill ran down Fiona's spine and her legs felt like jelly. She thought she'd pass out. "I have to go. Now. Otherwise Gilly will be sold."

"She is not yours to keep. You will change destiny."

"What does that mean?"

"Your actions will affect many lives. Some will live and some will die. Thwarted once, not twice, Gilly going forth the herd survives." Golden eyes pierced her soul.

Baa

Fiona cautiously turned her back to Eldar. No time to waste. She had to get busy. If Gilly couldn't fit through the turnstile then plan B, going through the weakened fence, would have to be the way out. She could kick out the weakened boards, just low enough to allow them passage, without the other horses being able to get through.

But let's not get ahead of ourselves. One thing at a time.

Tess and Tilda squeezed under the bottom fence rail and gave encouraged barks to Fiona and Gilly. Eldar hooted again.

That's interesting, he's not talking now. Has to be a vision or something...

Fiona unlatched the catch on the turnstile. She grabbed the gate and with difficulty moved it forwards and backwards, trying to loosen it. "Emmeric hasn't

used this in years," she said, more to herself than to any
of the others. She pushed and pulled, pushed and pulled.
With each movement the gate creaked and rotated more,
until she was finally able to make a complete circle in
one direction. She circled twice both forward and back-
ward. She was exhausted from the effort and hadn't even
left the property yet.

Fiona threw her backpack under the fence to the
other side and removed the duffle from Gilly's back, sliding it under the fence as well. Fiona led Gilly between the
forks of the turnstile. Gilly resisted and pulled back on
the lead rope. Fiona used the cue for Gilly to move over
and adjusted her rump into the opening. Gilly began
to paw the ground, obviously not happy with the tight
fit between the forks. She couldn't move an inch. Fiona
adjusted Gilly at a slight angle before pushing the forks
forward.

Her head was high in the air and the whites of her
large eyes showed. "Just a few more turns, Gilly. You're
almost there," Fiona said as she struggled to push the
forks forward despite Gilly's pushing back on the forks
pressed against her rump.

Gilly reared up, relieving the pressure that Fiona was
pushing against. The turnstile opened to the outside of
the pasture. Gilly came down on her forelegs. She pulled
the lead from Fiona's hands and bolted into the high

golden grasses of the adjoining property. Tess and Tilda ran after her. In a flash, the three were out of sight.

Fiona quickly rotated the turnstile to allow herself entry between the forks. She pushed with all her might and tumbled onto the golden grasses. "What have I done? This is a complete failure." Fiona lay on the grass looking up at the white puffs of clouds in the sky.

"As I said before, now is not the time."

"Don't discourage me, owl. You're just like Emmeric," Fiona snapped.

"It seems to me that you're more stubborn than the filly. You would do well to not just hear, but to listen when advice is given."

"You know nothing about me, Eldar."

"I know about the shadow in the vision that haunts you."

"That's impossible." Fiona curled up in a ball on the ground.

"So is a talking owl," replied Eldar.

Fiona got up and brushed herself off. In the distance she heard three voices. Girls' voices. But couldn't make out what they were saying as the warm summer air shifted the voices from being heard clearly. Fiona yelled, "Tess-Tilda-Gilly!" She yelled again, cupped hands beside her mouth, "Tess-Tilda-Gilly!"

The voices came closer. *I'll die if I'm discovered out here.*

Above the tall grasses Fiona spied a set of ears. Then a familiar face. "Gilly girl!" she shouted. Tess and Tilda came into view by the time she saw the whole of Gilly. Tess had a hold on the lead rope and Tilda circled the pair. Fiona swore that the dogs were smiling.

The girl's voices disappeared with the breeze. Maybe guilt playing a trick on her.

Fiona ran to the three and gave them all smooches. "Oh Tess, you're the best. Thanks for bringing Gilly back."

"You're welcome," said a smiling, tail wagging Tess.

Fiona hit the ground, passing out on the way down.

"Fiona, wake up. Are you okay?" mumbled several girls' voices.

She felt the slobber – dogs, and muzzle nudge – filly, before opening her eyes.

No, not girls' voices. I know better now. I'm listening to my animals.

Fiona stood slowly. She didn't know how long she was out. At least no shadow this time. And how could Eldar have possibly known about the visions? *Wise old owl, my butt.* And how is it that her animals were talking? No one would ever believe her. An overactive imagination combined with the stress of losing her family is what others would say. Not enough days in a life-time to answer these questions.

"One more thing before you go, since your mind is made up. I will make arrangements for some friends of mine to meet up with you tonight, where it is that you decide to bed down," Eldar said. "They will provide protection during the night. For the sake of Gilly."

"I have Tess and Tilda for protection," protested Fiona.

"You will need all the help you can get on your journey. Stubborn girl, take what is offered."

Emmeric, telling me what to do! "Okay. But how will I know?"

"Wings – fast and silent, slice through the night sky."

"Great, a riddle. But how will I know…"

"Beware of treachery." Eldar trailed off. "Beware of shadow." Those were his final words before closing his eyes and sleeping.

Fiona bent over to pick up her backpack. Gilly gave her a nudge, "I'm having so much fun. Can we do the round thing again, even though it was scary? What about my bag?"

Gilly watched the shocked look on Fiona's face. "What's the problem? Don't we have to leave?" Gilly asked.

"Yes, but I'm having a hard time with this talking

thing. I admit I'll enjoy the company more, knowing that we can all talk together like real friends. Maybe this is what it's like to have a nervous breakdown. That's got to be the explanation."

Fiona swung the duffle onto Gilly's back and tied the straps around her girth. She adjusted the contents of the bag that had shifted after being tossed under the fence. "That looks better."

"Feels fine to me," Gilly said eagerly. "I know I'm ready"

Fiona shook her head. *What's next?*

Tess grabbed hold of the lead rope between her teeth. Tilda fell in line next to Fiona and Gilly.

"We need a heading." Fiona pulled a compass from her pocket and pointed the group north-west. "Let's get out of these tall grasses so we can see where we're going. A deer trail is what we need."

They trudged through the golden grass. The sun beat down hot and the air was stifling. The warm breeze from before had vanished. The farm fields that they had to cross were massive from what she had seen on the Internet. But they would avoid towns and people and still get to the river.

"Fiona, we need to go home," Gilly announced. She was anxious and pulled against the lead rope, dragging Tess along.

"What's wrong?"

Pacing back and forth, Gilly said, "I need my mother. I don't feel good. What's going on? I'm not ready to do this."

"You're fine. You feel weird because you'd been suckling from Danuba. You haven't had any milk in a while. You're going to get through this – it's what's called being weaned. Trust me, you won't even think about it in a day or two."

But how would I know. I didn't think to ask Rose or Emmeric how long weaning takes. Drats! I hope she doesn't freak out.

"Let's find a stream and get you some water. You can graze for a while."

Tilda ran ahead. She returned about fifteen minutes later and dog yipped, then shouted in a girl's voice, "I found water. This way! Hurry. I found something else." Her voice trailed off as she ran ahead again.

"Tilda! Tilda! Come back," Fiona shouted. *I've lost my mind. Talking owls, horses and dogs. This is not happening! I'm not in Oz.*

Tess put the lead rope that she'd been holding between her teeth into Fiona's hand. "I'll go get her."

Fiona and Gilly ran after the two dogs.

The warm summer air picked up and carried voices again. Fiona recognized Tess and Tilda's voices – mixed with a number of very young voices and an occasional baa sound. She didn't know how many *animals* to expect. Gilly pulled Fiona, still holding the lead rope, up the crest of a hill. Below and in the distance on the flats they spied the dogs circling a small flock of sheep. It appeared to be about five or six black-faced Suffolks. Young ones, Fiona suspected. Not only had Tilda found a stream, but some sheep as well.

"I wonder who they belong to?" Fiona said. *I don't think there's a sheep farm for miles.*

Fiona and Gilly approached the flock, and as they did, the sheep panicked. Tess and Tilda responded by herding them into a tight group. The stream was behind the sheep. They had no place to go. However, the smallest one managed to slip out between the flock and dogs toward Fiona and Gilly as if not realizing they were there.

Fiona knelt on the ground in time for the little one to run into her. She grabbed the bundle of wool and fell on her butt in the process. "Hello there. It's okay, we're not going to hurt you." Fiona smiled. She petted the little one and introduced herself, Tess and Tilda, assuming the sheep would understand people talk.

"Do you have a name?"

"I'm – I'm Pip," the little one whispered, shaking with fright.

The flock listened to the exchange between the girl

and Pip. They relaxed and allowed Tess and Tilda to walk them to where Fiona, Pip and Gilly were. Fiona remained on the ground so that she was at eye level with the flock that numbered five. The rest were bigger than Pip. *Emmeric would call him the runt. I'm surprised the farmer let him live. He would say he wouldn't grow to his full potential and there would be no profit to be made. No good for breeding either. A few lamb chops is all, as Emmeric is fond of saying.* She cringed and felt sick to her stomach.

Two of the bigger sheep came forward and introduced themselves to Fiona. "Hi, we're Tan and Yan."

The next two came forward. "We're Methra and Tethera."

"Pleased to meet you. I'm Fiona and this is Gilly, Tess and Tilda," She pointed out her animals. "Seems to me that you five are a ways from home."

"We are," announced Yan.

"Can I ask why?" She was sizing up the sheep and noticed a distinction. Two sets of twins and then Pip, a single.

"I don't know if you know about our lot and our eventual fate? We need to protect Pip, if you catch my drift…"

Fiona leaned back and gave a serious nod. "I understand completely. We are in a sort-of-similar situation with Gilly. A matter of destiny that I had to take into my own hands."

Fiona let go of the contented Pip and released Gilly from her lead. Gilly nudged Pip toward the stream for a drink of water. The sheep gathered close around Fiona.

"Where are you headed with Gilly?" Tethera asked.

They seemed to speak as one. No real distinction in their voices. Fiona studied the four black faces. She sensed the worry and fear. She felt that she could trust them. After all, who would they talk to about her plans? They had run away too.

"We are headed north-west along the river. Legend has it that an old fort is up that way, in the north woods. We can live there, and Gilly will be safe."

Methra piped in, "May we join you on your journey? We need a leader and have none. This has been our problem. We can't decide where to go or how to get there without a leader."

"I don't know what kind of a leader I'd make. I've never done this before. I'm not even sure the fort really exists."

"We'll take our chances," Tan said.

She didn't commit to Methra. She dug a protein bar and juice box out of her backpack. The sheep grazed. Tess and Tilda settled under a grove of shade trees. Gilly joined them in slumber.

The sun was high overhead. Fiona didn't need a watch to know that noon was approaching. She was exhausted physically and emotionally and her head began to pound. This was so much more difficult than she could have imagined. And now the sheep wanted to join her small group.

This… is more stress than I can take. Do I need it? Really? Tess is the adult; I can't believe I'm saying this. I'll get her opinion.

A Matter of Poison

Jostles and nudges roused Fiona from a deep sleep. It felt the way it feels on a waterbed. You roll along with the action of the water, you have no control. She rubbed her eyes and thought for a split second that she was home at the farm. She forced her eyes open to see that she was completely surrounded by animals. As expected. They kept nudging and circling her, kicking up dust. They were impatient, ready to travel despite her need for: sleep.

Someone, probably Tess, had dragged the duffle and backpack to the spot where she lay. "Thanks, Tess." Fiona decided to no longer use the simple phrases when speaking to animals of "good girl" and "go fetch." Obviously they were capable of a decent grasp of the English language, picking it up from listening in to daily conversations on the farm. Maybe even from watching and listening to TV.

"Anytime."

"Tess, have you always understood human speech?"

Tess smiled. "I learned your language over the years as have most of the farm animals that care to learn. Some pick it up better than others, I have to say." She wagged her tail.

Fiona checked her watch. "Not too bad. We only lost about twenty minutes."

Bags adjusted, they were back on the trail. Tess and Tilda took the lead and were already out of sight. The sheep walked single file in a line behind Fiona and Gilly.

Tan cleared her throat. "Miss Fiona, what have you decided? Will you be our leader?"

Fiona turned around. "Please don't think of me as any kind of a leader. You may join us. I think if we work together we should be safe. But I can't guarantee anything. I hope you understand?"

"Perfectly. We thank you."

Little Pip in his soft voice chimed in, "We thank you, too."

Tess and Tilda ran back to give a report of what lay ahead. They'd already traversed a number of farm fields, which felt like miles, with no obstacles or difficulties. It had been smooth sailing. Fiona felt sorry for Pip as he dragged along at the end of the line – being the youngest and shortest in the group. Fiona imagined he'd have to take almost twice as many steps as the others.

"The tree line of the woodlands is some distance ahead. The river follows. We should avoid the woods our first night till we can figure out what, if any, dangers might be around," Tess announced to Fiona.

Fiona nodded. "Good idea. Especially for the sake of the sheep. Tess, scope out a safe place for us to camp."

"Will do. Come on Tilda. You're with me." Mother and daughter ran off in a northerly direction.

The longest part of the day had passed, and the golden light of late afternoon and the eventual dark of night were looming. Fiona felt the slow crawl of anxiety rise in her gut. Though she had gone on several campouts with the Girl Scouts, this was much different with a bunch of animals. *What am I, a Girl Scout leader?*

Gilly commented on Fiona's quickened pace and added, "I miss my mother."

"Me too, girl. I wish I remembered mine." *More than anything else in the world.*

The dogs returned with news. "We found an orchard surrounded by a stone wall. It should be a safe place for us to sleep, especially with the sheep," Tess said.

Tilda grabbed Gilly's lead rope from Fiona and the

two trotted off. "Tilda, don't go too ... Ugh, I sound like a parent. Tess, is it far?"

"Depends how fast we travel: horse speed, dog speed, human speed, sheep ..."

"I get it, I get it." Fiona chuckled at Tess's joke. *Hmm, another trait of dogs? They can be funny too?*

The group found a middle speed. On the cusp between warm, late afternoon and cool, early evening, Fiona watched as the dogs ran ahead for what she thought was a final scouting run to check that they were on course. And they were. Over a rise, the craggy tops of old apple trees appeared. The trees still bore leaves. "They're not dead. Maybe they still have apples?" Fiona said excitedly.

Gilly whinnied with delight and kicked up her hooves, just missing Pip. "I love apples."

"We need to talk about this, Gilly." Fiona stopped and turned to face her. She pointed a finger at her filly as she spoke. "You're not to eat more than one, maybe two apples at the most. And never any green ones. You'd get really sick and could even die!"

Gilly rocked back on her haunches. "Die?"

"From colic. Your intestines could... Oh, I don't expect you to understand. But you've got to really listen to me on this. Do you hear me?"

She lowered her head and ears, "I guess so."

Fiona spotted the apples as they neared the orchard. A blessing—food, and a curse—deadly. The stone wall surround appeared as they got closer. Gray field stones, stacked about as high as her shoulder. This wall was taller than the usual waist height on her. Typical dry stacked stone walls, as Fiona had come to learn, kept livestock in and intruders out. Or, in this case to keep livestock from the fruit.

Tan walked over to join Fiona and Tess at an old gate. Tan asked, "Are we going to be safe here, Miss Fiona?"

"Let's see. It looks rickety. But I think I can pull it closed." She grabbed hold of the wood gate, shook it free from vines and overgrowth and pulled so that it met the wall. Moss came off on her hands, a souvenir, which she was quick to clap loose from her palms. "We should be safe and secure tonight."

The sheep entered the enclosed orchard and began to clear the overgrown grasses without the need for Fiona to ask. Tilda asked Fiona, "Is it okay for Gilly and me to go play outside the wall, just for a while? Please? Please?"

"As long as you don't go far. I want to be able to see and hear you."

Tess agreed, "Maybe Pip wants to go along and play too."

Tan, Yan, Methra and Tethera gave hearty bleats of "yes," then heads down, resumed grass cutting.

Fiona watched; the sheep were very committed to the mowing project despite her worries that they would be a hindrance on the journey. Maybe they would be an asset instead. Even though it was only the first day—they had been no problem. Gilly and sometimes Tilda provided enough worries. But Tess was a big help. *I know I can depend on Tess.*

"Tilda, Pip let's play hide-and-seek. You two hide and I'll come find you," Gilly said. "Oh, do you even know what hide-and-seek is, Pip?"

"N-n-no," Pip said.

"We'll show you. Tilda, go hide, and I'll come find you."

"Why me? You go hide first."

"No, I'm the biggest." Gilly reared up to her full height.

"I'm older than you," Tilda growled. Then circled Gilly. And nipped her back leg.

Tilda and Gilly chased each other. Barks and snorts and whinnies carried throughout the orchard. Pip ran back to the stone enclosure as fast as his little legs could carry him to avoid the fight.

"Til-da, Gil-ly, get back in here!" Fiona was fuming. "Well, that didn't work out too well. What got into you two? And you've scared Pip."

Fiona bent down on one knee and cuddled little Pip,

who was crying, to calm him down before sending him back to the lawn-crew.

Tilda ran to Tess, head and ears down, tail between her legs. Tess gave her a prompt nip as punishment.

Gilly retreated back outside of the stone enclosure, galloping around the outlying trees and whinnying in a high pitch. She pawed the ground and roared. "I'm not wrong! I am the tallest. I'm not even a baby-foal anymore. I don't need my mother or anyone else. Fiona is not the boss of me!"

Gilly ran in circles around the outside of the walled enclosure. She snorted, jumped and kicked out. Only no one was paying any attention. "Great. No one even cares about me."

Fiona was busy attaching a blue tarp to an overhanging limb from an apple tree and gathering wood. She lost track of the young ones playing. The sheep cut the tallest grass under the direction of the dogs.

Gilly lowered her head, feeling sorry for herself and pawed the ground. Dust drifted up from between the dried out blades of late summer orchard grass. What she hadn't noticed till now were the handful of young apple trees around her—outside the walled enclosure. And there was fruit. "I love apples," she said gleefully. "Fiona did say I could have one or two."

No one is looking. Low profile—she slowly meandered

between the young trees and barely picked up her hooves so the others might not hear her, all the while eyeing the apples. Big round red ones. Green ones too. They all looked so good.

Gilly nudged and smelled the fruit. *Which ones do I want?* Yellow jackets buzzed around her head. *They must want the apples, too.* She moved slowly and found a branch at the right height for her teeth to grab hold of the sweet treat. *Good choice.* She bit into the crisp delight. Juices ran from her lips. Yellow jackets attempted to land on her muzzle but she shook them away. *Hmmm, to pick another.* She circled round the young trees, spying the choices within reach. Another red delight presented itself for consideration. It bounced along her muzzle and tickled her hairs. She expanded her nostrils for a whiff. Teeth caught it and pulled. A crisp crackle. Apple juice flowed. She shook away the yellow jackets. The game and reward of the taste enchanted her.

One more. One more. One more...

Tess, closest to the gate, noticed Gilly as she approached the orchard's stone enclosure. The filly walked slowly, head down, sweating and kicking at her belly. Gilly lay down, rolled back and forth, and moaned. Tess barked then yelled, "Fiona, Fiona—something's wrong with Gilly."

Fiona dropped the armful of firewood that she

carried and ran to the spot where Gilly rolled. Tilda ran with Fiona and arrived at the same time and looked at her mother and said, "What happened to Gilly? Why is she on the ground?"

Fiona and Tilda looked to Tess for answers. Tess could read the worry in their eyes. Tess warned Fiona, "Don't get too close she might kick out at you. She's in extreme pain. Colic."

Fiona trembled. Tess saw the look of panic on her face—hoping that Fiona would not have another attack and pass out. She nudged Fiona and licked her hand. "Fiona, you can do this…grab the medicine out of the duffle. Tilda, get the lead. We've got to get her up on her hooves. Quick!"

The two ran off and back in a matter of minutes. Fiona went to Gilly's head and hooked up the lead rope onto the halter. Fiona pulled and encouraged Gilly to her feet. Tess and Tilda nipped at her rear hooves. Up she went. But she began to fold her front legs in an attempt to lie down and roll. "Oh, no you don't, girl!" Fiona said. She pulled the lead to the side which forced Gilly to turn. She jammed the medicine tube in her mouth and squeezed. Most of it went in.

"You did a great job, Fiona. Now we have to keep her walking till she passes manure and her gut sounds are better. Tilda and I will take turns with you."

"How long?"

"This could take hours…"

Golden late day light was replaced with a purple horizon met by black moon lit sky above. Gilly was exhausted, as were the others. In a weakened voice she said, "I'm—I'm sorry. I didn't listen, Fiona. I was mad, and I didn't listen. I thought I could do what I wanted and that you were wrong about the apples. Why would they hurt me if they taste so good?"

Fiona brushed Gilly's forelock aside. "Gilly Girl. That's a hard question for me to answer. I don't know why good things can be bad at the same time. I can only tell you what I know and hope that it helps you to make the right choices."

Tess heard the honesty in what Fiona had said to Gilly and nodded in approval. *Fiona is growing up, wisdom—she will need this and more along the journey.*

Under star-lit sky they headed back to the safety of the walled enclosure. The sheep were huddled in a corner by the wall, fast asleep. It was too late to start a fire. Fiona pulled the rickety gate closed. An apple of all things would be all she would have to eat tonight. She barely had the strength to pull one from a branch hanging nearest to the tarp. Her hands were rope burned. Leg muscles and feet burned too from walking Gilly around. But she felt proud that she saved Gilly, and was happy for

Tess' words. Tess, Tilda, and Gilly settled along another wall in fresh cut grass, courtesy of the sheep. They fell asleep as soon as they curled into semi-circles on the ground.

Fiona managed one bite of the apple before falling into a deep slumber under the blue tarp. Dreams came quickly. Yowls and barks—danger—closer now, could not break through her dreams.

Night Terrors

Tess woke with a start, heart thumping.

Barks closing in. A pack of canines—not of her kind—approached from the east, out of the woodlands. The high pitch yowls woke Tilda who was now at her side, shaking.

Tilda whispered to Tess. "I've heard this before. In the distance at the farm. I never asked before. What is it?"

Tess put a paw on Tilda to keep her quiet. "Coyotes."

Tilda whispered, "They're getting louder. Are they coming this way? What do they want?"

"They hunt. They smell the sheep. Go wake Fiona."

Tilda ran under Fiona's blue tarp. She tripped over Fiona's legs and landed on top of her. "Get up! There's a big problem." With her teeth, she grabbed a clump of Fiona's hair.

Fiona pushed her away. "Geez, what the—"

"Hurry. We're in trouble. Coyotes!"

Fiona scrambled out of her sleeping bag. She ran with Tilda to where Tess stood. In Fiona's face she saw the recognition of danger. The yowls and barks were enough to creep anyone out.

"Tess. The sheep. What can we do?"

"Think, Fiona. How can you protect the sheep?"

Adrenaline surged through her body. She was fully awake and her mind raced. This was real danger. *Hold it together, Fiona. No vision, no vision. Not now! Don't let the stress get to you. What would Emmeric do?*

"Weapons. We need weapons. Tilda, round up and stay with the sheep. And bark—your fiercest. Tess, bark, too. SLINGSHOT. I've got the slingshot in the duffle. I hope we can scare them off."

The night sky provided some light, but not much. The moon was only half-full and the stars were out. Fiona's eyes were now accustomed to the dark—but she still tripped and stumbled over uneven ground and exposed tree roots on her way back to the tarp shelter. On her knees, she rummaged through the duffle and felt the cool metal of the slingshot. "Ah, got it!" She tore through the duffle in a panic. She couldn't feel the box of metal pellets – the ammo. "It should be here." It wasn't. Clothes and bags of food were scattered on the ground around her. "I need ammo…rocks!" She felt around where she knelt and picked up a fistful of pebbles and rocks stashing them in her pockets. She stood, leaving her knees dirty.

Fiona whistled for Gilly, who paced nervously in the orchard. "Fiona, I'm scared. I want to go home."

"Gilly, we need you too."

"I can't do anything."

"You can. You know what to do. Know how you kick and stomp when you're scared or angry?"

"Yeah."

"Use your hooves. Hard as you can. Front and back. Make it count."

The yowls and barks quieted.

Fiona's hairs stood up on the back of her neck. *They're here!*

Snapping her fingers and pointing, she sent Tess by the gate. Tilda had the sheep cornered on the opposite side where two stone walls met. Gilly stayed by Fiona's side while she bent down and hurriedly gathered more rocks, which she shoved into her pants pockets.

Fiona could tell that Tess stifled a growl despite the closeness of the coyotes. But Tilda couldn't help it. She growled, low at first more throatily. She barked, despite Fiona's snapping and pointing to be quiet. The sheep bleated. Then cried out, "Save us!"

Within seconds, the coyotes were on top of the stone walls. Fiona and her friends were surrounded by fierce white-toothed sentinels stationed along all four sides of the enclosure. Fiona quickly counted seven.

Fiona retrieved a rock from her collection, loaded the slingshot and fired.

A yelp rang out as a coyote toppled backwards off the wall. Fiona didn't know if she wounded the coyote enough to keep him away, but it seemed to enrage the pack. They descended into the enclosure. She couldn't even tell how many there were.

Fiona watched the pack chase the sheep that had by now gotten away from Tilda and scattered throughout. Pip stayed with Tethera and Methra who were on the run in a zigzag. Yan and Tan split up. Tilda looked confused. She didn't know who to herd first.

Fiona watched Gilly take note of one of the coyotes on a low, slow crawl toward Tethera and Methra. "Oh no, Pip! It's Pip he's after!"

What Fiona saw next shocked her. Gilly reared up and snorted in anger. She raced after the coyote that had his sights on Pip. She surprised the coyote from behind. Her front hooves came crashing down on him. Fiona heard the snap of bones and a sickening yelp.

Fiona turned to see Tess and a coyote locked in battle. Snarls, growls, white teeth flashing. She couldn't use the slingshot. She might hit Tess. Fiona's stomach clenched. It was hard to breathe. *No, not now. My animals—they need me. Please, don't let it happen.*

The stars overhead disappeared. Darkness spread toward her. Suddenly, Tess, Tilda and the coyotes stood still, heads cocked listening. Fiona felt something weird vibrating against her skin. The air changed. It got thicker and moved in waves. Was this a different kind of vision? Something like black clouds filled the sky. These masses moved in crazy directions. They came closer.

Maybe this is the end of me, and I'll be lost in the flames forever.

They were wings. Thousands. Maybe millions. Pitch black. Fiona couldn't see anything. She stood still.

All fighting stopped. The animals had stopped moving.

A high-pitch squeak sounded in her right ear. Something said, "Eldar sent us. He thought you might need some help."

"You're not a vision?" Something tugged her hair. She freaked out and wildly swatted her hands around her head.

"I'm Batavia." She was too quick for Fiona.

Fiona took a deep breath and shook off the panic. "Are you...a bat...bats?"

"No time for small talk. You've stumbled into their territory."

"They're after the sheep!" She felt her nerves again.

"They come here for the apples. But you brought them something better," Batavia said.

Colonies of bats dove like bombers onto the heads and backs of the coyotes. The high pitch squeaks from the bats made the coyotes cover their ears. They plucked at the fur of the unwelcomed pack of raiders.

Fiona couldn't see clearly what was going on around her. She heard Tess and Tilda bark incessantly. They too tried to cover their ears. Gilly snorted and whinnied. The sheep bleated. Black air moved all around her. Slicing through the night sky, as Eldar had put it.

The coyotes yelped and wailed. The bats really must have been hurting the pack animals. It didn't seem to take long. She heard the coyotes jump the stone walls to the outside of the orchard enclosure. Their yelps returned to barks and grew fainter. They had retreated.

Fiona felt relief and gratitude. She sat on the ground and cried her eyes out. This was an unbelievably close call. They could have all died—because of her. "Eldar was right. I'm not ready to do this. What was I thinking? Batavia, how can I thank you?"

Batavia flew loops around Fiona. "You may have

been ill prepared, but I think your heart is in the right place."

The winged black clouds flew off toward the field. The air stilled. Dim light of half-moon and stars reappeared in the orchard. Fiona said, "What should I do?"

"Get a good night's sleep. We will stay in the area till dawn, to make sure the coyotes don't return. You may call on me should the need arise—call my name," said Batavia.

"I will—we will. We've got to get to the other side of the river and make it to the old fort. That's going to be our new home. I don't know how long it will take, and I'm sure people are looking for us by now."

Batavia hovered in front of Fiona's face. "What old fort?"

She flew away.

Into the Woods

Gilly slowly opened her eyes. Not wide, slits. Enough to see the morning light at the horizon and darkness above. *Did I wake from a bad dream?* The yelps from the coyotes had been horrible. *Did I really crush the bones of one of them?* The wind rustled the leaves on the apple trees. The sound of apples falling was enough to send chills down her spine and make her ready to bolt. She was afraid that the coyotes were nearby. Looking around through slits—no bodies from the attackers lay about. Maybe they got away or were dragged away by the others in the pack. Her eyes widened in time, to see a group of small winged creatures, the bats, fly off to the west like rockets.

Everyone slept. But she felt pangs of hunger. She rocked forward onto her strong front legs and lifted her body up to full height. She shook her head to get rid of the leaves and grass that had found a home in her mane at night. Gingerly, she walked toward Pip so she didn't disturb the others. "Pip." She nudged and licked his ear. "Pip."

Pip stirred and gave out a soft *baa*. "What is it, Gilly? I'm sleeping. Come back later. It's still dark out."

"I thought you'd like to join me to get something to eat."

"It's dark out. No one else is up yet."

"Oh, come on. I'm starved."

"What about the coyotes?"

"They must be gone. I saw the bats fly away."

They walked away from the rest of the sleeping sheep. Gilly said, "I thought you were going to die. I sure hope Fiona knows what she's doing. The farm is much safer." She drew in a deep breath and put her head down to graze.

Pip didn't have as far to bend his neck to reach the ground. He grazed next to Gilly under the apple trees.

♥

Fiona stretched her arms out from under the sleeping bag and touched the now browned, partially eaten apple from the night before, and sent it rolling. Animals milled around and chomped on grass, except for Tess and Tilda who sat and stared at her.

"I know. You want to eat too." She rolled out of her sleeping bag. Her hair was a knotty mess and she still ached from last night's battle with the coyotes. The morning sun felt warm on her skin. She ran her fingers through her hair to smooth out the knots and pulled it into a ponytail. The bats were gone. "Ah, daylight."

She retrieved some dry dog food from the duffle bag. "That's it for now, girls. I'll have to hunt and—yuck— kill something for us to eat." The words were strange. *Kill something.* Like the way they were almost killed last night. The thought made her queasy.

"Batavia wants us to get out of here, pronto!"

Tess asked, "How far 'till we get to the river crossing?"

She hesitated. "I think we can make it today. Maybe. Or tomorrow." On foot, she was unsure of time and distance. The trip to the river crossing was easier by car. There were road signs and nice paved roads. No problems like coyotes wanting to eat your friends. It was different when you traveled by foot across farm fields and woods. Nothing was where you thought it should be. It wasn't as if she had the advantage of flight. If she were a bird she'd see in the distance and head directly to the crossing.

The terrain changed. Farm fields gave way to woodlands. They were further away from where people lived. But they might still come across hikers and campers. Too early for hunters. They'd come in the fall. She had camped out with her Girl Scout troop somewhere around here. It all sort of looked the same. *Is this journey really a good idea?* Doubt surfaced in a big way after the coyotes last night. She waved a hand in front of her face, waving the thought away. She'd keep calm for the sake of her companions. *No sense in getting everyone upset.*

She took her compass from her pants pocket and readjusted their direction north-west. North to make sure they didn't head back toward civilization, and west would eventually be the river. Finding the foot bridge would be tricky. *Why didn't I think of this before? I'll call on Batavia tonight and see if she can help spot the bridge.*

Tess looked at Fiona and wagged her tail as if in agreement. You didn't need words for everything. Fiona spotted a low stone wall. Not as tall as the one that surrounded them last night. This one was knee high. Gilly, Tess and Tilda ran ahead and jumped it with ease. The others looked worried. Sheep had short legs, especially Pip. But Pip appeared carefree.

"Not to worry, gang. We'll get you over the wall," Fiona said.

"Tess! Tilda! Come back. I need you."

The dogs jumped back over the wall and waited for Fiona's command. "I'll get the front feet onto the wall.

You nip and push to get the back feet up and over. Yan, let's start with you."

Together Fiona and the dogs lifted and pushed the sheep over the wall. When she got to Pip, Fiona bent over and scooped him up in her arms. She sat her butt on the wall and swung her legs up and over in one motion. "There we go," she said smiling, lowering Pip to the ground.

Everyone celebrated their crossing with cheers. Fiona covered her ears. The voices were overwhelming. In the chaos of the noise she couldn't make out what was being said.

"Okay, you all did a great job. Let's take a break."

At least *something* was going right for a change.

Gilly took more notice of the views and terrain. They were a big change from the gently rolling pastures and farm building that she knew. No more views to distant pastures with the familiar sounds and smells: horses, cows and sheep. What lay ahead limited her sight. The trees were scary and lots of them. Not like the two in her pasture that provided shade and kept the flies away. *I can't see anything but trees.* No end in sight. They were big and the rustling sound the leaves made was too much to bear. The low hanging branches reached out to grab her. They were big monsters with gnarled fingers.

No more soft, sweet grasses under hoof that you could nibble whenever you felt like it. No swoosh of grasses; instead, irritating snaps and cracks of twigs and branches. It was hard to walk on. Leaves covered young shoots of grass that had a bitter taste.

The branches on the ground hurt her hooves. "Ow. Ow." She held her head high and perked up her ears. She pawed the ground and whinnied. "I want to go home. I want to go home."

Fiona took Gilly's lead rope and snapped it to the halter and jerked on it. With a firm voice she said, "No, Gilly. We've come too far to turn back."

"The monsters will get me in the woods."

"Calm down, girl. I won't let anything happen to you."

Tess said, "Let's keep moving before we run out of daylight." Everyone else was in good spirits and appeared to have enough energy to keep going despite Gilly's meltdown. Tess took the lead and carefully picked her way through the oak and beech trees. The exposed roots and fallen trees made walking dangerous. It would be easy enough for Fiona and Gilly to sprain an ankle or leg, as they were tall compared to herself, Tilda, and the sheep. Being short had its advantages. She navigated around the trees and obstacles, all the time watching the progress of the others. Mindful of Gilly's fragile mental state, she kept a watchful eye on Fiona and Gilly in the hopes that the filly would not spook and bolt while Fiona held the rope.

She thought she smelled something familiar, off in the distance. Something man-made. A light breeze gently rustled the leaves. And there it was again—that smell. Her nose twitched high in the air. She'd smelled it at the farm.

"What is it, Tess?" Fiona said.

"I smell something familiar."

"Good or bad?" Fiona trembled.

"That all depends." Tess identified the smell. "It's a road."

"We'll have to cross it," Fiona said.

They walked on. It was an easy walk for Tess and Tilda. There it was.

"Everyone stay here. I'll go ahead to make sure the coast is clear," Fiona said. She handed the lead rope to Tilda.

Tess came along with Fiona. They climbed up a slope from the woods to the side of the road, staying low so as not to be spotted if a car came by. She listened for the sound of traffic. There was none. She whistled for the others to join them. They quickly ran across and down the slope on the other side. Still no cars.

"I'll go back up to the road and try to figure out where we are."

"Good thinking," Tess said.

Fiona was gone a long time. Tess was not worried. But the others were restless and milled around. Tilda, Pip and Gilly moved nervously among the trees. Yan, Tan, Tethera and Methra wandered around in a loose cluster, heads bent to the ground. Not much grass to eat.

Fiona reappeared. "Cool beans! I found a sign. We're not all that far away—by car that is. We have to re-adjust our course for the woods—but we're okay." She slid down the embankment to where the others waited.

"What sign?" Tess said.

"For the camping area and footbridge at Craggy Frog Bottoms. Then we take the river split to Green River and that should eventually take us to the fort." She sounded excited.

Fiona was glad that today was a good day. They were used to the long walks and even the woods weren't all that awful—except for Gilly. The weather was great. None of the animals misbehaved. She knew that they'd eventually come across a man-made trail the closer they got to the river.

The sky turned golden, and she felt the air cool. The

sun danced with the treetops. Her stomach rumbled. *No time for food.* Nightfall was not far off. A quick glance at her watch confirmed this. They'd better call it a day while they were deep in the woods. They were almost there.

She had no idea how long it would take to find the fort once they crossed the river and made it to the split. She bit her non-existent fingernail. It had to be there. She had a mission, and nothing would stop her.

Not Expected

Fiona debated whether or not to make a fire. *Why bother? To roast an apple?* The thought of having to kill something still made her stomach roll. It might come to that. She had protein bars and dried fruit, but she'd have to conserve the supply since she didn't know how long it would take to reach the fort.

Tess gave Fiona a look and nudged her with her wet nose. "Tilda and I are going for a run. We'll be back shortly. Why don't you go ahead and make a fire to keep warm? I know we'd like it when we get back."

"Don't you want some kibble first? You girls did a lot of walking and guiding today."

"No, wait till we get back. And wait for us before you eat."

"If you say so." Fiona didn't know what was up with that request.

She busily checked on Gilly and the sheep while gathering fire wood and setting up camp. Gilly complained even though the sheep grazed quietly. "There's nothing to eat!"

"Sorry, girl. I didn't count on the grass being so thin. Get out from under the trees and look in the sunnier spots. See?" She kicked away the leaves that covered a grassy spot, discovering a good patch.

Gilly pawed at the remainder of the leaves and grazed.

The sky darkened to a pink-purple. The only noise Fiona heard besides birds was the sound of sheep and Gilly chewing. *Where were Tess and Tilda?* The fire felt great, but her stomach rumbled from hunger.

The dogs appeared, each carrying something in their mouths. Fiona's eyes widened. *Oh, gross me out.* The dogs lay two dead rabbits at her feet. Tess wagged her tail and said, "We hunted. You cook."

Fiona retrieved her knife from her backpack and looked at it. She felt guilty for what she was about to do.

Gutting the rabbits, she held back on barfing up an empty stomach.

The smell and blood were gross. She held her breath and squinted as much as possible while keeping dinner at arm's length. Emmeric butchered rabbits all the time, but Fiona tried not to be around. She could never get used to the blood and guts. She hesitated. Then cut. It was jagged. Emmeric would have been mad. She singed the fur off over the flame. The stench of burnt fur was unbelievably horrible. *How can I even think about eating this? I'll give it to the dogs.*

The smell got better as the rabbits roasted, like when Rose cooked steaks on the grill back at the farm. She didn't feel grossed out any more; just really hungry. Her stomach growled. Tess and Tilda sat patiently on the opposite side of the fire. Fiona watched the dogs drool through the flame. "Soon. Real soon."

The rabbit tasted delicious.

Full bellies—falling asleep snuggled in front of the fire—heaven.

Fiona woke and stretched her arms and legs. Her mind felt clear and focused. "Rabbit is great. I feel great." They got underway after eating and packing up camp. *The bridge today.* None of the animals complained except for Gilly walking over the branches. "Ow, ow,ow."

Fiona snapped. "It's not worth it. Gilly can go to another home for all I care! She's a pain in my butt." She took some calming breaths. *But Gilly is big...and would be the hungriest...and is so young.* She shook her head, ashamed at her own words.

The dogs ran ahead. Tess took in the aroma of water. The river. She spotted what she thought Fiona was looking for. A wooden bridge. Wide enough for people and animals. *Why would anyone walk over it?*

Tess reported back to Fiona on what they'd discovered. "Fiona, I think we found your bridge."

"Really? Great!"

"I don't know about that. I can't see why you'd want to cross it."

"Of course we want to cross it. Otherwise we have to swim across the river. The water is too deep there."

"If you say so," Tess said.

Fiona raced ahead, jumping over branches and tearing through the underbrush. Tess saw the look of horror on Fiona's face as soon as she spotted the bridge. "No! It can't be washed out!" She fell to the ground and moaned.

Pip came over to Fiona and snuggled his way into Fiona's lap and licked her face. Tilda and Gilly joined in to give a hug. Pip encouraged, "Don't give up, Miss Fiona."

"We have too," she wailed. "The bridge is no good to cross. There's no way to get over." She hiccupped a sob.

Tess spoke up. "You're not a quitter. Don't give up now. There has to be another place to cross up-river. You've overcome a lot of obstacles and dangers. Look how far we've come."

"I can't do it."

"You can, and you will! Stop the pity party," Tess said.

"Remember you said how important family is. Aren't we your family?"

"Yes. I love you all…let me catch my breath." Tess watched. Fiona wiped her eyes and face with her sleeve. She took several deep breaths then laid on her back, seeming to stare at the sky. Pip and Tilda laid across her legs. Gilly played with Fiona's hair with her lips.

Tess listened to Fiona scold Gilly, "Stop it."

"Fiona, I promise I'll stop complaining," Gilly said.

"Do you mean it?"

"I'll try my hardest. I don't want to be sent away to another family."

Tess grabbed Fiona's shirt sleeve. "Let's get going."

♥

Fiona watched Tess and Tilda take the lead west along the river bank. They were out of sight but she could clearly hear them rustling the leaves up ahead. The footing was softer thanks to a mossy path, making the trek easier on the sheep and Gilly.

Let's see how long before she begins complaining.

Shadows began to lengthen in the woods and the bright light of day turned golden. Another night was approaching. Fiona wondered if the dogs would hunt for rabbit again.

I have to be realistic. Maybe they were lucky last night.

I can't expect a feast every night. Stomach, we may have to settle for less. Keep it to a low grumble.

Cousin

"Sunrise…wake…eat…walk…rest…eat…walk…camp…eat…sleep…night."

Fiona was sick of listening to the chant from Gilly, Tilda and Pip. They circled and fell to the ground and sang out, "Are we there yet? Are we there yet?"

Fiona glared. She felt her face redden and clenched her fists. "Knock it off!" This was so Junior High. She hated being teased in school for being the new girl; no i-Pod, no cell phone and forced to wear homemade dresses sometimes. Rose and Emmeric were *Little House on the Prairie* old-fashioned, and had no idea how bad the teasing got from spoiled-rotten classmates who had everything. She couldn't take the mocking from her own animals.

I won't cry. They can't make me cry. Why would they do this to me when I'm trying to help them?

Tess came to Fiona and licked her fist. Fiona knew it was the mother in Tess that wanted to comfort. "I need a friend right now." She bent down and threw her arms around the dog's neck. "Thank you." She buried her face in Tess's soft fur.

"Fiona, they are children. Don't let them get to you."

"But it hurts."

"I know. Remember why we're out here."

"Thanks, Tess. I'll try."

Fiona didn't want to admit that she had lost track of how many days they were away from the farm. She looked at her watch. The chant sung by the others was fixed in her mind, and she repeated it to herself. There had been a lot of sunrises and sunsets, come to think of it. Three-four-five? She picked up a flat pebble, threw it into the river and watched it skip along the surface.

Same river. Right direction. Got to cross it at some point, as they headed west.

Had she already missed an opportunity? It was never right—too wide, too deep or too much current.

Gilly, Tilda and Pip ran ahead. They ignored Fiona's, "Get back here…" Her voice trailed off.

Gilly dared Tilda and Pip, "Let's race. Come on, whoever gets to the bend in the river first, wins!"

"What are we going to win Gilly? Fiona will be really mad and tie us up," Tilda said.

"There's no way I can beat either of you, so why bother," Pip said.

"Come on! It'll be fun."

Gilly raced ahead and looked back at the others. Pip was last, as usual. Gilly's hooves no longer hurt. She was used to the sticks, branches and rocks. Ahead and out of sight of the other two, she came to a dead stop. "Wow, what's that?" She snorted and smelled the air. Her ears perked up and her eyes widened. "Come on, hurry, you've got to see this…"

Tilda and Pip caught up, "Geeze! What is it?" They stared into the distance.

Gilly figured she could show off her smarts. "It's falling water."

Tilda said, "It looks dangerous. How are we going to cross the river, much less continue on this side of the river? Now there's a big mountain in our way with water shooting out. We better go back and tell Fiona."

"They'll catch up soon enough. Let's have some fun and play. Enjoy our freedom," Gilly said.

Pip said, "I don't like the looks of the falling water. It's scary."

"Well, I suppose if you look at it a certain way, it does look like something with wings and a head and body," Gilly said.

"I know what it reminds me of," Tilda said. "Those

buzzards that fly over the farm, looking for a dead meal. Emmeric calls it road kill."

"Gross!" Gilly said.

"Well, doesn't it?"

"I suppose so."

Pip had turned to go back.

"Don't go Pip. Honestly, everything will be okay," Gilly said.

The three watched the falling water. It crashed on the rocks and water below.

"What's that?" Pip said.

Ripples in the water zigzagged their way.

"Look!" Pip shook with fear and backed away.

The others looked as a wave of water headed toward them. Something, a yellowish-green flowed at the top of the water. Gilly said, "We'd better back away from the edge. Must be some water animal."

The three backed into the woods and hid among the bushes but kept their eyes trained on the mysterious thing. It swam fast. From the moment they first spotted the wave, it took minutes for it to reach the shore. The wave stopped. The yellowish-green stuff disappeared.

"We'd better stay in the bushes till everyone gets here," Gilly said.

They huddled together.

Gilly heard the clop of hooves and the clearing of

nostrils. "I wonder who's here? Has Danuba escaped from the farm and tracked me down? You two stay here. I'll go see who it is."

"Be careful," Tilda said, followed by a throaty growl. Pip cuddled even closer to Tilda for protection.

Gilly stepped out from the bushes and tip-hoofed toward the horse sounds. She peeked out from behind a tree and spotted something that was far from being Danuba. A horse stood facing the water and shook as if to rid itself of pesky flies. Water dripped from its yellow-ish-green mane. *The water animal! Not a water animal. A weird horse...*

The horse turned as if it had read Gilly's mind. Its eyes swept the woods to find her partially hidden behind a tree. The horse's eyes traveled toward Gilly's back half and twitching tail. It smiled, a sly smile, in contrast to its beautiful features.

Shivers ran up and down Gilly's spine. *Warning!*

Water flew off its fur. Greenish-brown fur that shimmered. Its mane continued to drip water. Gilly's eyes widened with panic. *It doesn't smell right.* Gilly backed away, her hooves in motion.

"No need to run," the horse said. "There's nothing to be afraid of, young Gilly." It smiled.

"How do you know...my name?" Gilly stuttered.

"Don't be shy. Come closer, cousin."

"Cousin? What are you?" Gilly stepped back.

"I am a horse, same as you. I am your cousin in a manner of speaking." The green-brown horse bowed to Gilly then strutted in its entire splendor. "Come closer."

It's fur glimmered. Gilly felt drawn to the beauty of it. By what? The eyes. The eyes were hypnotic. A soothing voice drew her forward. Several steps forward. The eyes were yellow.

This isn't normal. I don't want to, but I can't resist getting closer... I need to see it up close.

Gilly perked her ears and concentrated on the voice. A stallion. Gilly walked towards the horse. "You never said how you know my name?"

"I knew your mother, knew when she was in-foal with you. I knew what the girl Fiona named you. The moment she named you."

"How could you?" Gilly got closer. "That's impossible!"

"I have the Sight."

Tilda, from the bushes, broke the spell that she was under. "Gilly, no! You're too close, get back here!"

The green-brown horse turned, galloped, and then dove into the river.

Gilly raced back to Tilda and Pip as if her life depended on reaching them.

Kelpinore

Fiona kicked up dust and rocks on the path. "The nerve of Gilly to run off with Tilda and Pip. I'm done. Finished! When I get my hands on her she'll wish she was never born."

"Fiona! You sound like Emmeric," Tess said.

She felt her face flush. "You're so right Tess. Thanks for reminding me. I need to develop patience!"

"Don't you think I had my paws full with Tilda? Thank goodness I had Rose and Emmeric to help me raise her. And, you too. I don't love her any less despite the trouble she gets into. Oh, trust me, she's going to know all about it when we catch up to her," Tess said.

"Do you think the sheep will scold Pip?" Fiona said.

She and Tess glanced at the sheep. They nodded their heads. The heat of anger left. She took big strides in the direction that Gilly and the others had gone in. It was nice to know she wasn't the only one feeling this way.

♡

Tess cocked her head, ears alert. She heard the sounds before Fiona could.

Fiona stopped in her tracks and concentrated to make out the noises. Branches snapped and stones clapped. Soon she heard hooves, barks and bleats.

"Sounds like the wayward three."

"Fiona, Fiona!"

She knew Gilly's voice by heart. She stood with her hands on her hips, ready to lace into Gilly. Tess nudged Fiona to be patient. "Wait for an explanation first."

She nodded and relaxed her arms by her sides.

"You need to see what we saw! It's amazing, and we can cross the river…"

Fiona put her hands in the air. "Slow down, calm down. See what, exactly?"

Tilda blurted out. "A horse!"

"Sort of," Gilly said.

"What is sort of? What is it? And you found a place to cross?" Fiona's heart jumped in her throat. "What did you see?"

Gilly answered. "It was a kind of horse. It was spooky."

"Why would a horse be spooky to you?" Fiona said. "Was it a big stallion or something?"

"Well yes, a stallion, but weird."

"Did you eat something that made you sick?"

"No, Tilda you tell her."

"It didn't look right. I don't know what else to say… oh, and it swims under water."

"Hmmm, maybe it was…" *What about that dream I had. No. Water Horses don't really exist? But this journey has been strange.* Fiona rubbed her chin. "If that's the case, I hope it moves on." *Clever. I bet they made the whole thing up.* "More importantly, you found a place to cross?"

"Yes, before the falling water," Tilda said.

"You mean you found a waterfall? We can't cross there. The water will be too rough."

"The falling water is in the distance. The water swirls. Then there are big rocks. And then it's calm again," Tilda said.

"This has to be it. And don't think you're off the hook for running away." Fiona stared at the three with her mean look and then glanced at her watch. *It's already four p.m.* She shook her finger at them.

♥

The dirt and grass path changed dramatically. She stumbled over loose rocks along the river bank. She kept her arms outstretched for balance. The sound of crashing water came from ahead. Around the bend, there were huge boulders which did seem to calm the water from the falls that looked pretty far away. No way to guess at the distance. *They didn't make this up.*

She stopped short and gasped at the shape of the waterfalls. A dark hollow of rocks with two wings of water crashed to the rocks below. Fear ran down her spine. *A buzzard. Not a good omen.* She tore her eyes away from the falls in panic and scanned the rocks. There's no way they could climb over the boulders. She studied the water and depth where it was the calmest. *Not too bad. I think Gilly can touch bottom most of the way.* The river was still wide here.

As shaken as she felt, she forced her mind to form a final plan. Every day she had run scenarios in her head of how they would cross if given the chance. *I'm not worried about the dogs. They can paddle across. The sheep should have some buoyancy. Pip, I'm not sure of...maybe he can ride on Gilly. Gilly should be fine as long as she doesn't panic...the sheep can surround Gilly like life-jackets...I'll walk and swim holding Gilly's lead rope...*

"Fiona!" Gilly yelled.

Fiona turned to see a creature swim from the falls

in their direction. It was big. And then it was gone. *My Loch Ness Monster! For real? Is it a Water Horse then?*

Fiona heard hooves on the ground behind the trees. She caught a glimmer from between the branches as an animal, the likes of which she'd never seen before emerged.

Fiona backed up to where the dogs stood. They growled and barked and ran in front of Fiona to protect her. She backed more to the sheep who were circling in terror. Gilly walked out in front of Fiona to face the intruder. *Gilly had told the truth.* Fiona continued to shake with fear. Her animals made so much noise she covered her ears and closed her eyes, hoping that it would go away.

The glimmering horse stepped from the trees into the open. "Ah, if it isn't cousin Gilly and my friends Tilda and Pip. So good to see you again, so soon. And you brought the human girl and others. Splendid."

Gilly stepped forward and pawed the ground, snorting.

"Such a brave little cousin." The horse stood in full light. The sun reflected off of its green-brown shimmery coat. Too bright to stare at. It shook water from its coat and mane, but water continued to drip. "That feels better."

"You never did say who or what you are." Gilly felt bold.

"You are so charming, little one," the strange horse chuckled.

Gilly felt the lure of the stallion take over. Yellow eyes. Gilly shook on purpose, which seemed to break the spell. "Who are you?" she demanded.

"Manners, manners."

"We don't have time for you," Gilly said.

"Ah, yes. Your little journey. Can I be of assistance?"

Gilly knew that she wasn't making any progress and a glance back confirmed what she had felt; Fiona was scared stiff, as were the sheep. The dogs had their teeth bared and continued to snarl and growl, awaiting a command from Fiona to attack. Gilly hated the way the stallion knew too much.

"Shall we start over?"

Gilly lowered her head. "Very well."

"As this is my home, guests go first," the stallion said.

"My name is Gilly. But you knew that. You already met Tilda and Pip." She pointed with her muzzle. "Tess is Tilda's mother. Fiona is my human girl, as you say. The sheep are Yan, Tan, Tethera and Methra. We found them along the way with Pip."

"Splendid, then. My name is Kelpinore."

"What breed of horse are you, anyway?" Gilly kept her stare away from Kelpinore's strange eyes.

"A mix of draft horse, if you must know."

"Why do you swim all the time?"

Kelpinore laughed, "I'm a horse that loves water."

Gilly knew that Fiona was in a hurry to cross the river and this was probably the only place safe enough to do it even though she had her own fears of crossing. Gilly looked at the water.

"Yes, I sense your hesitation, cousin. I would be more than delighted to help in any way I can." The horse smiled. "I can swim. And I so enjoy a dip and romp in the pool by the falls to cool off, even under water."

"But that's not natural." Gilly's legs wobbled and she was ready to bolt. She looked back to see if Fiona had recovered. Fiona snapped out of what looked like a trance. Gilly ran to Fiona who patted her neck and said, "Don't look at its eyes. It does something weird when you look."

Fiona nodded in agreement and held on to Gilly's mane as the two walked toward the stallion. Fiona turned to Tess and Tilda. "Keep an eye on the sheep."

Tess said, "Be careful. I don't trust it." She continued to snarl and bare her teeth.

Gilly and Fiona walked slowly toward Kelpinore.

The horse was beautiful. Fiona had never seen

anything like it before. Even with a rainbow box of crayons and a coloring book she colored all of her horses' shades of browns and grays. This horse shimmered like glitter. The green-brown fur was amazing. Must be from the river's water. And the mane was a yellowish-green. *But the eyes! Yellow eyes? Oh quick, look away.* Fiona edged forward slowly with Gilly beside her, hands gripped firmly to Gilly's mane.

A distant whisper came to Fiona's head.

Strangers…be careful.

Hadn't Rose said this? When Fiona first came to live with the Quimbys? A shopping trip, to the mall outside of Springfield? No,… well yes, Rose had told her not to talk to strangers. Rose had felt uncomfortable in crowds and insisted that Fiona not wander ahead. But someone else had said it in her head. Another woman's voice was saying it now. She halted and closed her eyes, keeping a firm hold on Gilly. In her mind she saw two red braids dangling down the front of a purple shirt. Sneakered feet peddled along on a tricycle. She saw the single front wheel and white basket attached to the handlebars. Purple and white streamers flapped in the breeze by her hands. The trike raced along the sidewalk. An ice cream truck was parked at the end of the block.

Couldn't it be me?

My memory?

The woman's voice said, "Stop." Fiona looked back to see the lower half of a woman. She was wearing a pink dress and white sandals. Fiona didn't see her face. A little girl's voice said, "Ice-cream. Ice-cream truck."

"Wait for me," the woman said. "There are people we don't know by the ice-cream truck. Don't talk to strangers, Fiona!"

Mom!

Fiona opened her eyes. Tears streaked down her face.

Crossing

"Hold on tight, Fiona. I don't trust it, either."

Fiona's hands trembled, and something had made her cry as they approached the horse called Kelpinore. Gilly wondered about that.

"Come now, I'm not going to bite." Kelpinore smiled then pawed the ground. "That's better. Perhaps I can be of some assistance to you. It looks as though you've got your hands full, Miss Fiona."

Gilly halted, which forced Fiona to stop walking. Gilly felt they were at a safe distance. She watched Fiona use her shirt sleeve to wipe away tears. Fiona tightened her grip. "We can manage."

"I'm more than ready to lend a hoof or my back." Kelpinore whinnied a laugh. "Look, there are eight of you. Please let me help."

"That's okay. I have a plan."

Oh, Fiona, why are you telling it things when you know you shouldn't. Fiona, turn and walk away. Now!

Gilly nudged Fiona and began to back up.

"Manners, Miss Fiona. I have merely offered my services for which there is no fee – as you might say," Kelpinore snorted. "I can carry you and the little sheep. Why won't you consider my offer?"

Gilly knew what the snort meant. The snort signaled its frustration. She had done the same when she didn't get her way. She nudged Fiona even harder, sending her off balance. Fiona caught herself. The stallion was trying to trick Fiona into trusting it.

Think fast, Fiona!

"Kelpinore, where is your herd?" Fiona asked.

"Ah, I am but a herd of one. However, I would love some company...Gilly?"

Gilly pawed the ground.

"Where were you born?" Fiona asked.

"Miss Fiona, considering we've just met, these are rather personal questions," Kelpinore answered.

Fiona studied the horse and put her mind to work. "Maybe I can help. You were banished by your herd. An outcaste. For being different?"

Kelpinore reared up and snorted in a rage, then took off.

Fiona and Gilly turned and walked away.

"It's a good thing you pushed me back there," she told Gilly. "I was in a sort-of-trance. We need to cross. And that horse, as beautiful as it is, is creepy."

This is almost like my dream. Rose told me about Water Horses in Celtic lore. They trick children into climbing onto their backs and you can't get off. Then they take you down into the water, and drown, and eat you...

"You should feel creeped out. I'm a horse and I don't trust it. Cousin, my rump," Gilly said.

Tess wagged her tail. But barked ferociously. The wag for Fiona, the bark for Kelpinore "Thank goodness you came back. We were all worried about you and Gilly so close to that horse. He's not normal."

"I hear you," Fiona replied. "Tess, big problem. Kelpinore wants to help us cross the river. He's willing to carry Pip and me. I made him mad, so he's probably changed his mind now."

"You can't even consider..." Tess said.

"No, you're right. But we need to create a distraction, something to get rid of him," Fiona said.

"Tilda and I can chase him, nip at him. Bite, if we have to. That should send him away."

"I'm not sure if that will work. He might attack us when we'd be vulnerable in the water," Fiona said.

Tess looked at the sheep and rolled her eyes. They

had sorrowful looks on their faces. *Sorrowful looks meant no help there.*

All of a sudden Pip broke away from the group and ran through Fiona's legs. Just out of her grasp. "Pip, come back here!"

Pip bumped right into Kelpinore. "Sorry...I..."

"Apology accepted, little Pip. I'm glad to see someone around here has some sense." Kelpinore lowered his head and pushed Pip up onto his back. "Comfortable? We'll be on the other side of the river in no time. Hold on tight."

Tess watched in horror. Kelpinore turned and galloped toward the pool of water before the falls. A wide-eyed Pip turned to look at his friends. He appeared glued to Kelpinore's back. The stallion dove in, taking Pip with it. The yellowish-green mane showed near the surface, zigzagging toward the falls. No one spotted Pip.

Fiona screamed with all her might. "No, Pip, No!"

Tess held her back from bolting toward the water pool. "Fiona, he's gone. He's gone!" Tess tightened her grip on Fiona's pants leg. The pants ripped.

Fiona ran toward the water.

"Fiona, this is our chance. Pip created the distraction we needed," Tess said.

"NO! We have to save Pip!"

"Pip must have known what he was doing. The poor thing," Tess said.

"I won't give up on Pip." She turned toward a stunned Gilly. "Gilly, I need you to find Kelpinore...pretend you want to join him."

"Me?" Gilly whinnied and paced. "I can't."

"You can do this! Play up to his vanity. That you want to join him too," Fiona said.

Everyone gathered around Fiona. "We all need to work together to save Pip." The sheep and dogs nodded. "Hmm." Fiona rubbed her chin. "Better yet Gilly, tell Kelpinore that you'll stay with him if he turns Pip over to us. I'm sure he'd prefer your horsey company."

The sheep baa'd.

Gilly stepped back and said, "Hey, I'm not staying with that creep!"

"Gilly, we're playing a trick on him. I'm not leaving anyone behind." Fiona turned to the sheep. "Girls, we need you to be super brave for Pip. Yan, organize the rest to create confusion around Kelpinore so that Pip can escape. Like when the coyotes had us surrounded, break-up and scatter and then come back toward Kelpinore from different directions. He won't expect that."

Fiona knelt and petted Tess and Tilda. "I need you

two to nip, herd him away if possible, attack if all else fails. I'll use the slingshot."

Fiona paced and looked at her watch. Gilly had been gone for about three hours and Fiona dreaded that Gilly too was being held prisoner. The sheep circled in a tight bundle with Tess and Tilda holding them in even tighter. They could cross now, but the two young ones who needed saving, the ones who the journey was all about, were gone. The sky above clouded gray, covering the late day golden sun. Fiona's mood grayed as well.

Tess and Tilda bolted toward the bushes, ears perked forward. Fiona's funk lifted as she ran to the dogs. Finally, Fiona heard two sets of hooves clopping toward them. Around the corner came into view Gilly, Pip and Kelpinore. Kelpinore had a haughty, high and mighty head. Whereas, Gilly and Pip looked down at the ground.

"Is it a swap, a truce then?" Kelpinore said. "Gilly is to live with me?"

"Just one question, where is your herd?" Fiona asked. She didn't want to run into any more horses like him.

"Oh, them. Humph. North-as-you-go at the big stones. But they won't care for the likes of this motley pack of human and lower-level-beasts." Kelpinore smiled a sly smile.

Fiona put her hands on her hips. "I hate when

animals talk in riddles!" She whistled. "Lower-level-beasts do your thing!"

Yan and Tan were first to reach the wide eyed horse. Pip took his cue and ran to Fiona. Tethera and Methra circled to Kelpinore's rear forcing him to kick out. Tess and Tilda each nipped a front leg. Fiona shot a rock at the big horse's rump. He turned and kicked like a mad wild bucking bronco. Fiona tried not to laugh. They had to get him to run off. Kelpinore opened his mouth and tried to bite Methra but Tilda bit him on the side of his face, a dangerous move. He screamed in pain and shook his head wildly. He kicked out and twisted his body at the same time. Fiona shot a rock at Kelpinore's neck. He flew up into the air, landed on all fours and then bolted for the water. He dove in and must have swum under water, as he was not spotted again.

"Let's get out of here," Fiona said.

"Pip, let's float you onto Gilly's back. There you go. Yan, Tan, get on Gilly's right side. Tethera and Methra left." She pointed out the positions. "Tess behind Yan. Tilda, you're behind Methra. Nip as needed to keep them moving."

Fiona held the lead rope at some distance so that Gilly wouldn't kick her with her front hooves. They moved slowly into the river.

Tess admired the way Fiona had pulled herself

together. "Everything is good back here. Tilda, are you okay?"

"I'm fine."

Fiona stepped cautiously on the submerged rocks. She looked ahead in the water for the shallowest spots. "Is everyone okay so far?" She rocked sideways, arms outstretched to keep her balance.

Tess answered, "Everything looks good from here." She could see Fiona and Gilly slipping on the wet rocks. Pip trembled. Fiona was waist deep in the river and held her arms and the lead rope in the air. Gilly stretched forward, head extended, snorted, and pinned her ears back. Tess smelled fear settling in and told her, "You're doing great, Gilly. Almost there."

The sheep squeezed closer to her and could barely touch anything below, trying to keep their heads above water. The dogs pushed and prodded the backs of the sheep with their noses. *Almost there. Keep them going, Fiona.*

Fiona slipped and jerked on the lead rope. Gilly panicked and almost lost her footing. She scrambled to regain footing. Her front hooves went up in the air. Helpless, Tess watched as one of the hooves came down and smacked Fiona in the back of her head. She went under water. Tess bounded past the sheep and grabbed the back of Fiona's shirt. She dragged her to shore where she lay on her back.

Tilda grabbed Gilly's lead rope, and swam, pulling her and leading the sheep to land. They dragged themselves onto dry ground and shook the river water off.

"Is she dead?" Tilda asked.

Gilly ran in circles. "I killed her. I killed her."

Tess put her nose to Fiona's face. "No, she's not dead. She's breathing. She'll come 'round."

Despite assurances, the sheep, in a clump of wet smelly wool, shook and cried.

Where There's Smoke There's Fire

Fiona saw the bedroom from her vision. She recognized the big flowers on the old torn wallpaper. *This is my bedroom. This is the new house in the new town in Agawam Point.*

A towering dark shadow approached. "What do you want?" she asked nervously. *The flames are next.*

A voice answered. A boy's voice. Not a bogey-man. "Fiona, we need to get out of here. "Hurry!"

Flames licked up the walls behind the boy shadow. *He knows my name.* Who is he? The smoke curled into the bedroom. It thickened and she coughed, wrenching her stomach. Her throat tightened. She backed up to the window and felt the fresh air behind her. There was no good way to escape from the boy shadow or the flames. Just the window.

The boy coughed in fits and pushed against her. "Jump! Jump!"

She couldn't see his face. The voice seemed familiar. *This is happening too fast. I can't figure it out. I need more time.*

He kept pushing. She felt her body squeezed through the window. Like being folded in half. Felt the fresh air. Felt the ground and the pain. Then felt nothing.

In her mind she heard the boy. "It's all my fault." He was close to her on the ground. "I have to go away..."

She heard muffled voices first then felt herself coming round. Then she felt the pain in back of her head. She mumbled, "Boy, boy..."

Clouds and branches spun in the sky when she tried to open her eyes. Her face felt wet and had warm tongues all over. She pushed at the air in front of her face and felt fur. Eyes opened – Tess and Tilda. "What happened? The fire...where am I?"

Tess said, "You're with us."

"What happened?"

"We were crossing the river and you slipped on the rocks. Gilly's hoof hit you in the back of the head."

"When did that happen? I don't remember a thing."

"A while ago."

"What about the fire?"

"I don't know anything about a fire. Don't you

remember Kelpinore took Pip and we were trying to get away from him and cross the river to find your fort?"

"I remember." Fiona sat up slowly. "How is everyone?"

"We're all good. We took turns looking for food and eating while you were sleeping."

Fiona got up off the ground slowly. "I'm still dizzy."

"We better not travel far, just enough to get away from Kelpinore and this place."

"Inland then. Away from this river. We still have to find the Green River."

"What were you saying before about a fire and a boy?" Tess said and cocked her head.

"I'm not completely sure." She rubbed her chin. "I'm still trying to figure it out. It has something to do with my parents dying in a fire. My life before Fairfield and the Quimbys adopting me. By the way, where's Gilly?"

"She's been hiding because she thinks she killed you."

Fiona cupped her hands to her mouth. "Gilly! Gilly Girl!"

Gilly walked slowly from the woods, head drooped and ears down.

Fiona forced a smile. "You really are a lot of trouble, but this time it wasn't your fault, it was mine."

Gilly approached Fiona and nuzzled her. "I was so worried. Are you okay?"

"My head's killing me and I'm a bit dizzy." She put

her hands to her head. Dried blood had matted her hair. "I don't think I can go very far today anyway."

"You'd better not carry your bag, put it with the duffle on Gilly," Tess said. "Tilda and I will take turns with the lead rope. You just walk as best you can."

"I know they say Border Collies are really smart, but you really are and wise, too." Fiona chuckled, making her headache worse. She grabbed her throbbing head. And held tight to Gilly for balance.

They traveled away from the river, in a northerly direction. The woods thickened. Fiona looked up. The canopy formed by the trees blocked the gray sky. It was hard to see what was hidden under the leaves. Fiona knew that Gilly wanted to complain. The filly licked her lips and snorted. Her hoofs connected with tree roots, and made a cracking sound.

Tess and Tilda had to hop over stumps and roots zigzagging. Fiona watched where they stepped and tried to follow the same pattern. She couldn't afford any more falls.

The sheep had the most difficult time. They were especially slow. They too had no choice but to continue on this journey over difficult terrain for the sake of Pip. But Fiona couldn't bend over and do any lifting to help them along. Not with her aching head. The sheep pushed themselves over obstacles and out of unexpected animal holes in the ground. Tess and Tilda took turns to encourage them along.

Fiona looked around. There were no landmarks. She'd forgotten to look at her compass when they left the river. And now she couldn't see the sky. Checking her pockets, it wasn't there. *I must have lost it in the river when I fell.* They were deep in the woods and she was feeling defeated and in pain. She looked at her watch. The face had been smashed. She didn't know what to tell her friends. *Now I've gotten us all lost. Stupid, stupid me.* She sat on the ground to rest, and stared up at the green canopy. *How far have we gone?*

Tess twitched her nose first. Then Gilly put her head into the air and flared her nostrils. "What do you smell?" Fiona looked around.

Tess hesitated with the answer. "Smells like a fire."

"Which way?" Fiona didn't smell anything other than pine needles and rotting leaves.

Tess walked to the right, or east by Fiona's reckoning. "Maybe we should see what it is."

I wouldn't mind running into some hikers at this point, since we're so lost anyway.

"Whatever you think," Tess said.

They walked long enough that the canopy opened to a darkening sky signaling the approaching end of another day. The terrain had become steep, mountainous. The air cooled. She spotted now darkened mountain peaks in the distance. They were away from any of the river valleys, in the mountains now. Did they miss the Green River? Everyone was tired and quiet. Fiona listened to the rustle of leaves and the cracking of hooves, against partly buried roots. She stopped and sniffed harder.

"Tess, is it my imagination or do I smell smoke?"

"It's not your imagination, you do smell the smoke. It took you long enough." Tess smiled and wagged her tail.

"Well, I don't have a super sniffer or sonic hearing like you all do."

"I can't help it that you're human. You should be more like us dogs." Tess woofed.

Fiona enjoyed the new banter with Tess. It was like having a girlfriend or big sister on the journey. Suddenly she didn't feel lost. It didn't matter that Tess had fur and four legs. Being with her friends—her family—made the pain bearable.

The smell of smoke got stronger. *Don't freak out. You're not in the bedroom.* It floated up high in the air and filtered down under the now opened canopy and held its place at nose level. "Looks like a clearing up ahead and a huge mountain range beyond to the north."

Fiona motioned to Tess that the two of them would scout toward the clearing while Tilda stayed back with Gilly and the sheep. They were far enough away that her animals shouldn't be heard by possible people at a camp site.

They made their way carefully, listening for anyone or anything. *No more Kelpinores.* She gulped back her fear.

"A little further. I can see the clearing and barely something off in the distance. Tess, what do you see?"

"Looks like a…I don't know what you'd call it. Nothing I've ever seen before. A building of some sort. Not like the farm."

"Could it be the fort?" Fiona asked.

"How would I know? It's huge."

"Do you see anyone? *Anything*, actually?"

"Not yet. We need to keep going," Tess said.

Now in the open, Fiona crouched to make herself smaller, and the two crept along. A meadow with overgrown brown grasses spread before them. In the distance, a sprawling gray stone structure with fairy tale like towers came into view.

Destination Unknown

"That can't be the fort. It's like a castle. Out in the middle of nowhere!" Fiona said.

"How did it get here?" Tess asked.

"It's not Indian and doesn't look French. It's too fancy to be out here in the middle of the mountains. But not as fancy as the Disney Castle. This can't be the place the Ward woman discovered. And by the looks of things someone must be living there." Fiona pointed. Smoke from a chimney curled into the darkening sky. "That's what we smelled in the woods, not a camp fire."

"Why would they have a fire going this time of the year? Emmeric burns wood in the winter when it's cold outside," Tess said.

"You're right. The only way to find out is to go and see who's living there."

Tess gave Fiona a look. "This might be the end of our

journey. They'll probably give Emmeric and Rose a call saying that they found you, and us for that matter."

Fiona looked down at the ground. "I suppose you're right. It's probably just as well. We're lost anyway. I lost my compass in the river and smashed my watch. I really don't know where we are. And the food's almost gone. *Nothing but granola and apples. And the thought of you and Tilda chomping on raw bunnies and squirrels is gross.* Rose and Emmeric will be so angry with me anyway. They'll un-adopt me, send me away and who could blame them. At least they make money sending Gilly away."

"Fiona, you've done a good job so far," Tess said.

Fiona sighed. "My mind's made up. Go get the others. We'll head for the castle and surrender. Our journey is over."

They waded through grasses taller than the sheep. They didn't say a word or ask any questions. More of the castle came into view. It was massive. Not tall like a fairy tale castle but spread out. It was made of gray stone and a darker gray slate roof. Two towers anchored a center section. *I wonder if Sleeping Beauty or Rapunzel are home?* Chimneys protruded from various levels of the castle. *Neat! This must be really old. I bet that's how they used to heat the place.* Fiona quickened her pace toward the castle. She wondered what they might see and was relieved to find shelter at last. She loved old buildings and making discoveries. Like the time she snuck into an abandoned farm house down the road from the Quimbys and found an old tea cup decorated with delicate pink flowers. She brought the tea cup home and hid it in her Memory Box along with the hospital I.D. band from Mass General and the paper from the Social Worker with her Agawam Point address on it, in the back of her closet. Rose would have said that, stealing is stealing when it's not yours to take. And besides, the tea cup played no part in her life, past or present. She snuck back into the old farm house and returned the cup.

The closer they got, the more interesting the place. The center walled section had a huge arch and opened to a cobbled courtyard. "How romantic. Look at the old fountain in the middle!" Fiona hurried forward.

Tess grabbed her pants leg to slow her down. "Wait, Fiona. Let's go slower. We don't know who or *what* to expect."

Fiona opened her eyes as if for the first time and saw details that she had missed on their approach: The castle was pretty dilapidated. "Oh, no." She stopped walking, and had mixed up feelings of enchantment and fear. "I hadn't noticed…the chimneys are falling apart. The roof is open in a lot of places…birds are getting in, windows are broken. Look at the vines all over the place." *There shouldn't be anyone living here!* A tingle ran down her spine.

"So why is there smoke coming from one of the chimneys?"

"It's as if you were under a spell, a trance. Not seeing the place for what it is." Tess blocked her. "That's the second time that's happened to you. Need I remind you of Kelpinore?"

"No, I'll try to be more careful. Keep an eye on me, though. I don't trust myself. We need to figure out who's in there."

She turned to Tilda and told her to watch Gilly and the sheep. "None of you make a sound and keep low in the grass until Tess or I call for you. Understood, Gilly?" She pointed at each individually.

Gilly nodded but there was fear in her eyes.

Tilda asked, "But if you don't come back…what should we do?"

Fiona gave a shooing motion. "Try finding your way home. And I'm sorry for all the trouble I've caused."

Fiona ran toward the castle. Tess caught her pants. "I suppose I should call out when we get to the courtyard… or should we sneak around? I don't want to give some old bum a heart attack. I can't imagine anyone living in there, well, except maybe me." Excitedly she pointed to the arch and courtyard. "There must be some good parts of the castle to stay in."

"We'd better figure out what's going on before you start redecorating the place."

"Oh, Tess." She smiled and the gray cloud of defeat she'd been feeling lifted.

They reached the massive stone wall and Fiona touched it. The feel of cool stone was absorbed into her warm hands. "This is really neat. How is it we found a real castle? Not some worn down fort? This is way more than I thought we would find. This has been such a weird journey. Why not!"

She slowly peered around the side of the arch into the courtyard, careful not to make a sound. She listened for signs of human life, but there were none. A bunch of chickadees and sparrows were picking seed heads from the weeds between the cobbles. The structure continued around to the right and left, connecting on the opposite side to a central three-story house.

"Look, the towers that we spotted. And lots of stables." She recognized them by uniformity, though most of the doors had rotted away years ago. They formed a horseshoe back to the arch. "Those bigger doors are where they would have stored coach wagons years ago. I wonder if any are still inside? It's too dark for me to see from here."

She began to walk toward them. Tess grabbed her again.

"Sorry, Tess. It's so enchanting. I can picture how this looked years ago. I bet it's from the early 1800's, maybe the 1700's. Like ones I've seen in books. I wonder what happened? Who could let this place go to shambles?"

Another tingle ran up and down her spine. The hairs on the back of her neck stood on edge.

Territory

Eyes watched the girl and dog from the dark recesses off the courtyard behind stable doorways. Nostrils flared.

"We have guests. Ronan, tell the others to prepare," Magnus said in a deep voice. He pawed the ground and flared his nostrils again.

"Yes, Magnus." Ronan, second-in-command, bowed to his leader. His black mane covered his eyes. He had learned well over the years to never question Magnus's authority. This assured his survival.

"Well, what are you waiting for? Take Lorcan with you…and make sure that our human is not seen," Magnus grumbled and curled his upper lip. "Lorcan, the hoods…eight…no, make that three."

Ronan was a good soldier, but his standing would surely slip away. The arrival of Lorcan earlier in the spring sealed his fate. *If only Brora hadn't bore Magnus a son.* Lorcan ran ahead of Ronan. Ronan snorted and flared his nostrils at the youth.

♡

"Tess, I feel like we're being watched." Fiona felt a chill and goose bumps rose on her arms. "I don't think my chill is from the stone wall."

"I feel it, too." A growl rose deep in Tess's throat.

"It makes sense with the smoke that we saw."

"What should we do? Go to the courtyard? Knock on the front door? Shout out?" Fiona said. Her voice trembled.

"Let's take our chances in the courtyard and see if the watcher comes to us," Tess said.

Fiona grabbed Tess's ruff and held on. Her hands shook. *So much for confidence.* The two walked slowly through the arch toward the fountain. The flock of birds flew up with a whoosh.

Fiona gasped.

You could hear a pin drop.

Gray shadows were cast in front of the stable doorways.

"If anyone's watching, we're sitting ducks."

Exposed. Fiona and Tess stood still and listened…

Creak, creak from inside a stable…Clop, clop, clop from a doorway.

Fiona felt dizzy. Her breathing tightened. *Don't pass out. No visions. No visions.* She grabbed Tess even tighter.

Tess stood on Fiona's foot and licked her free hand. "Steady, Fi."

Fiona's eyes widened as a massive creature emerged from the shadows of a doorway into the gray of the courtyard.

"A horse!" she screamed. "We won't hurt you. Good… boy?" She reached her hand out, palm up, though the horse stood some distance away. "I assume you talk too, since every other animal has spoken since I left the farm."

The huge brown and white horse flared his nostrils. He snorted and vigorously bobbed his head, and pawed the ground.

Fiona understood his body language—this is *his* turf. She and Tess had trespassed— *his castle.*

"Sorry to bother you. We're lost. I'm Fiona, and this is Tess." She patted her friend on the head.

"So?" Magnus' voice echoed around the courtyard.

Fiona stumbled back. *He could be as dangerous as Kelpinore.*

"Who travels with you?"

Tess gave Fiona a look.

Fiona wanted Tess to read her mind. *I don't think lying is going to help. He's bound to hear Gilly or Tilda if they get bored and act up.*

Fiona thought to ignore his question. But it was no use. He would find out and soon. "There is another dog, Tilda, five sheep, Yan, Tan, Tethera, Methra and Pip and a weanling, Gilly."

Magnus's eyes lit up. "A weanling? Colt or filly?"

Fiona hesitated. "You never did tell me your name?" She couldn't believe she had the nerve to ask. He made her so nervous.

"Bring the others! Bring me the weanling! Do it now!" he bellowed, ears pinned back.

Two more big horses appeared from the shadows and stood by his side.

"Tess, I think we're in big trouble…" Her shoulders slumped in defeat.

The closer the horses came, the bigger they got. Fiona staggered back, nearly falling over Tess. "Oh, my…!"

Tess growled and bared her teeth, tail curled in the air and hackles raised. "Fiona, this isn't good."

"How do you know? Maybe it's because we invaded their territory. I get along with animals – most of the time. I can reason with them." She looked at her feet. *I think, maybe.*

"No. These horses are different. They're wild. They're not domesticated."

"What about the smoke? Someone had to light the fire," Fiona said.

"I know," Tess said.

"You two, come closer," Magnus said.

Slowly, Fiona and Tess approached. The horses were huge. Fiona guessed eighteen to nineteen hands tall. Her mind swirled. *What breed? Some type of draft horses. The feathering. The colors: brown, black and some white. Shires maybe?* Her thoughts evaporated in a poof.

"Are you a complete idiot, girl? Answer my question." Magnus said.

"I…I didn't hear you."

Magnus snorted. "How did you find us?"

"By-by-accident?" Fiona trembled. Her knees almost gave out. "Honestly. I don't know how we found this place. We followed the river and got lost. We didn't mean to find you…I mean, we…"

Magnus turned to the other two and whispered something that Fiona couldn't hear. Tess tilted her head in concentration.

"Ronan! Lorcan!" Magnus yelled.

Within seconds two more horses appeared. One as big as Magnus and the other was adorable. A weanling by the looks of it. Bigger than Gilly. The tail was the right length for its age—about five or six months. Fiona couldn't tell if it was a filly or colt. She wasn't close enough. They approached Magnus with cloth things hanging from their mouths.

Fiona squinted to see better. She thought she'd wet her pants. Terrified, she squeezed her legs together and grabbed Tess even tighter.

"Ouch." Tess shook loose from Fiona's grip.

"Sorry."

"No talking, you two." Magnus turned to the other two horses that had originally come out of the barn with him.

Fiona still couldn't hear what was said. In a flash, they kicked up dust and headed out through the archway, where her friends waited, unaware.

Fiona gasped. "What are you doing?" She spun around toward the archway.

Magnus showed his teeth and pinned back his ears. "Being the perfect host, girl."

Fiona was not fooled by his body language. He lied. She'd been around horses long enough to know deceit. When a horse is about to do something different from what you want, they always give it away if you watch for the signs. Gilly always gets wide eyed and puts her head up, swishing her tail before bolting away. A game she liked to play to avoid capture.

Her friends were about to be captured this time. Terror gave way to anger. "Leave my friends alone!"

"What kind of host would I be? I want you all together, safe and sound." Magnus followed with a whinny.

"I doubt it," Fiona said. She put her hands on her hips.

Gilly and Tilda trotted into the courtyard followed by the sheep who shuffled in their wake of dust. Two sentry horses prodded the sheep forward.

"Fiona, isn't this great? We're saved!" Gilly shouted.

"Shush, Gilly."

Magnus chuckled. "Your weanling is right. You have all been saved and are in safe company. Gilly, you say? By the looks of it, your filly is about the same age as Lorcan. Splendid. And you travel with food. This is all just too perfect," Magnus whinnied.

"Food?" Fiona looked at the sheep. "No, you have it all wrong. They are my friends."

"Don't be so short-sighted, Fiona. I understand lamb is a delight for humans and even dogs to eat." Magnus glanced at the dogs. He gave his sentries a look and snorted out a command.

The sentries herded the sheep toward the stalls. They looked at Fiona with pitiful eyes. Her stomach wretched.

"Tess, Tilda, stay."

Janet L. De Castro

"Now that was sensible. Do you have restraints, what you call leashes, for the dogs?"

"Yes," Fiona mumbled.

"Let's find a comfortable place for the dogs to stay."

Fiona rummaged inside the duffle bag on Gilly's back. "Here they are." She snapped the leashes onto Tess and Tilda. "Sorry, girls."

"It's okay, Fiona." Tess licked her face. Tilda did too.

"Ronan, the hoods."

Ronan stepped forward. Two burlap hoods dangled from his mouth.

"Put these on the dogs."

"Really? Why is that necessary?" Fiona said.

"Just do as you are told," Magnus said.

"Yes, Emmeric!" Fiona said.

"What was that?"

"Nothing." Fiona adjusted the hoods over Tess and Tilda's heads.

"Lorcan, the hood."

Young Lorcan walked timidly toward Fiona with the hood between his teeth. His head was down as he approached her.

"Head up, eyes alert, Lorcan," Magnus said.

Lorcan snapped his head high.

Fiona couldn't help but feel sorry for the little guy.

"It's okay, Lorcan," Fiona said softly, putting her hand out toward him. "Good boy."

"Get on with it, Lorcan. Girl, don't touch him."

Fiona sneered at Magnus before taking the hood from Lorcan. She put it over her head. *Drat this fabric's too thick. I can't see out.* She listened to the vanishing clop-clop sound of horses leading Tess and Tilda away.

"Lorcan, take Gilly to her new home," Magnus said.

Gilly didn't even so much as say good bye. The two horses trotted off, probably to play. Fiona stood alone with Magnus in the courtyard. She'd lost everyone. Even Gilly went away so easily with the stranger colt.

Fiona heard the clop of Magnus's approach. He nudged her forward, and she tripped on a cobblestone. "Hold my mane," Magnus said.

She reached up and grabbed a silky clump, surprised at how soft it felt for such a horrible horse. Fiona picked her feet up higher than normal to avoid tripping over the stupid stones. Magnus directed her to the left, she supposed around the fountain, and toward the house. They stopped. Magnus whinnied.

A pair of hands grabbed Fiona's arms. Not big, calloused hands like Emmeric's and not small, soft hands like Rose's. Somewhere in-between. These hands worked.

She gasped. "Who are you?"

Lorcan

"Come on, Gilly. Let's play," Lorcan yelled. He ran circles around Gilly and jumped in the air. They were in another courtyard on the other side of the castle.

She was alone with this stranger colt. Her nerves gave away her fear. She danced sideways and cried a shrill squeal. "What about Fiona and my friends? I can't leave them behind."

"Don't worry about them. They're fine. It's our time. Time to have some fun. That's what horses are supposed to do." Lorcan approached Gilly and they blew into each other's nostrils. Gilly knew that Lorcan would smell her fear. "Really, Gilly, I'm not going to hurt you. No one here will. You're one of us."

Gilly stopped her nervous dancing around. *Lorcan sounded reasonable.*

"Let's get those packs off." Lorcan nodded his head

toward her back. "Why on earth are you carrying human sacks? That's the girl's job, not yours."

"Really? Where I come from, horses carry humans and pull carts, too. That's what we train for. That's our job."

"Humans don't control us. We take care of ourselves." Lorcan grabbed the cinch strap with his teeth and pulled the packs free. They fell to the ground with a heavy thump.

"Fiona will want her things," Gilly said.

Lorcan harrumphed. "She can come get them herself." He pawed at the packs as if they were an annoyance. "Your head restraint, you call it a halter...we'll work on that later. In the meantime, come on. I'll race you to the top of that hill." He threw his head high in Gilly's direction and swished his tail.

Gilly spun around on the sand-covered cobblestones and slipped. She regained her footing but Lorcan was already ahead by four lengths, and he had longer legs. She galloped all-out to catch up. Her nostrils flared, and she blew air out sounding like a horn.

Gray clouds floated by in the darkening early fall sky. An evening breeze picked up and played with their short manes as they ran. Gilly felt a freedom she had never felt before with this extraordinary looking colt. Gilly also felt a damp chill. Rain was on the way. *At least we have shelter and maybe a new home, according to Lorcan. What could be better?*

Gilly refocused on the race. But Lorcan had beaten her without question. He pranced on the knoll of the hill, under a tree, rearing up to his full height. "Victory is mine."

When she played with Tess and Tilda and even Danuba and Lileana, the winning wasn't so important. The winner and loser shared in the victory, and they laughed together. It was all in fun, not competitive like now. Winning mattered too much to Lorcan. She wasn't laughing.

"Lorcan, I've had a long day. Where can I bed down?"

"Oh, come on. I'm having fun."

"Another time," Gilly said.

"Okay, if you insist. I'll take you back to the stables, and you can meet Brora."

"Brora?"

"My mother," Lorcan said.

"Is she nice?"

Lorcan shrugged. "I don't know. She's just my mother."

They walked back to the castle and into the main courtyard. Clopping sounded from a number of horses. *I hope his mother is nice...*

They entered a stables area that felt cozy and smelled

good, too. Gilly inhaled the fresh smell of straw bedding, as clean as Quimby Farm. *How is that possible? There's no Rose, Emmeric, or Fiona to care for the horses and stables.*

"Hello there," whinnied a voice.

Gilly approached the voice slowly, with head lowered. She turned her eyes up.

"Come here so I can smell you."

A beautiful mare stood before her. She had a black mane and was brown with a white blaze on her muzzle and white socks and feathers on her legs. *This must be Brora.*

"Hello," Gilly said in a soft voice.

"Come closer. I won't bite."

"Mom, this is Gilly," Lorcan said.

"Well, aren't you just darling. Remind me, what breed are you, my dear?"

"I'm a Haflinger," Gilly said.

"So you are. Such a petite girl. I take it you're still a weanling?"

"Yes," Gilly replied.

"How tall will you be when you are done growing?"

"My humans say around fourteen hands, whatever that means."

"You have humans that control you?" Brora jerked back.

"Well…yes. I guess," Gilly said.

"Oh, you poor thing. You'll never have to worry about that here."

Gilly stood before the massive Brora and they blew air into each other's nostrils. Brora began grooming Gilly with her teeth and pulled some burrs out of her flaxen mane. Gilly groomed Brora's side with her teeth—she couldn't reach much higher. Brora seemed really nice. *I miss Danuba and Lileana and the Quimby humans. I wonder if they miss me.*

"I hope you will think of this place as your new home and us your new family."

Gilly didn't know what to say. She liked Brora. Lorcan was a show-off. Magnus and Ronan were plain scary. She needed to talk to Tess and Tilda. *Tess is smart. She'll give me advice.*

Where's Fiona?

Someone

"Get your hands off me!" Fiona tried to shake free, but the grip of someone's hands on her arms got stronger.

"Take her to the west tower. You know the room," Magnus said.

Someone shoved her forward. Fiona was terrified not knowing what was happening. "Stop pushing me."

"Step up," the male voice said. "Step-step-step-step." They were going up. It had to be into the house. Fiona felt coolness on her face, though her back was still warm from the last of the heat outside.

They walked inside. The sound of their feet hitting the floor echoed. *Maybe a stone floor.* A big space? She focused on her hearing since she couldn't see through the hood and couldn't feel anything since someone held her arms behind her back. ...*Two-three-four-five-six...*

"Who are you?" Fiona asked.

"Walk," was his only reply. He prodded her forward again.

"Hey. Don't be so, Pushy!" Fiona was angry and shook one arm loose from his grip. She reached to feel for obstacles that might be in front of her. She didn't dare turn on her captor, he sounded like he was taller, and older. She lost track of her steps forward. Her hand landed on smooth rounded wood. A railing.

"May as well keep it there for balance," Pushy said. "Step up-step-step-step…"

The steps were uneven and felt well worn, but solid. Definitely stone. They wound round and round as they climbed. Fiona felt dizzy and unsure of her footing. She stumbled and grabbed the rail. "Can't I take the hood off so I can see where I'm going?"

"No. I'm watching out for you. I'm not going to let you fall."

Fiona relaxed despite the situation. She was listening to Pushy's voice. It was disguised. *Count the steps. I keep losing track.* She sighed, but Pushy did not respond. They reached a landing and walked to the next set of stairs. Up and around.

"I'm dizzy, can we stop?"

"At the landing."

They rested briefly, and then walked. Up and around. *Three. That's where I am. Three floors up. In the west tower.* They stopped. She felt Pushy's free arm brush along her side. He had reached forward. She heard the squeak of a heavy door open.

"In you go." Pushy gently shoved her.

Before she could take the hood off and swing around to see him, the heavy door slammed shut. The door lock clicked. Fiona banged on the door with her fists. "Let me out! Come back, come back. Who are you?"

She turned away from the door to see the room for the first time. Fiona clapped her hands to her face. "It's amazing!"

The room was huge with tall ceilings. Not like her small, simple bedroom at Quimby Farm with well-worn furniture. This old furniture was shiny and looked like it had been waxed. Like stuff you see in books. A four-poster bed with drapes. A fireplace. Dust sheets on the couches and chairs. Carefully, she removed the cover from the bed and was amazed at how clean the bedding appeared. She bent over to smell the pillows and bedspread. *Not even musty.*

"This looks like a room from a mansion."

But these fine trappings didn't ease her worries for her friends. Would the sheep go to slaughter? Would Gilly forget about her? Would the dogs be killed? Worry lead to a rip-roaring headache. She kicked off her shoes and eased onto the bed. Yawning, she was overwhelmed with a desperate need for sleep after the journey they had taken. "I'll just lie down for a few minutes. Hope that helps my head."

The sound of roosters crowing seeped into Fiona's sleep. She stretched out. *I don't remember getting under the covers.* She smelled the remains of a wood fire from the fireplace. Eyes still sticky from sleep, she spotted the backpack and duffle bags lying on the floor, partly under the bed, and a tray with food placed on a chest. "Huhh?" In a panic she pulled the covers over her head. *This has to be a dream. Did Pushy come in here in the middle of the night?* Screaming in anger, "Who are you, show yourself."

Fiona threw the covers back and jumped out of bed. Her hair looked like a bird's nest covering her eyes. She pushed it back and out of her face. Fiona ran to the big door and tried to open it. It didn't budge. She pounded with her fists. "Hello, hello. Let me out of here!" She pressed her ear to the door, and heard nothing.

She slumped to the floor and felt like crying. *No, I won't cry. I won't give in.* Thoughts traveled to Rose and Emmeric. Are they even looking for me?

♡

The sounds and smells in the farmhouse at Quimby Farm were never the same after Fiona's departure. No more lavish farm breakfasts – instead oatmeal and toast or fruit and cereal. Rose couldn't bring herself to enjoy cooking family meals now that it was just she and Emmeric. Scraps went to the chickens – no Tess or Tilda eagerly waiting under the kitchen table. No barking dogs. No daughter running down the stairs. Rose listened to the sobs coming from Fiona's room upstairs. "Emmeric, honey!"

No reply.

Rose climbed the staircase and called down the hallway, "Emmeric?"

"I'm here. Still trying to figure out the computer." He blew his nose. "It's so slow, now I see what Fi-Fiona was complaining about."

"What are you looking for?"

"I'm checking our Fiona Facebook site and the other missing per-persons sights to see if there've been any sightings or-or…anything. I forgot again how to get to favorites. Can you show me? This computer stuff is so frustrating. I just want her back home!"

Rose put her hands on his shoulders. He heaved a sob. "Emmeric, we'll get her back. I'm sure of it." She felt an empty pit in her stomach.

He turned in the chair to face her. His eyes were red.

"It's my fault. I was too strict. I didn't see that she needed teen things. I guess I treated her like an employee instead of a daughter. Was I was afraid to love her and be a father?"

"It's a balancing act, dear." Rose tried to smile. "We can't spoil our daughter. And we can't afford to give her *everything* she asks for. Belonging to our family means responsibility on her part too. We're a family and need to respect one another, and work together. Fiona needs to respect that we are her parents and above all else that we love her and want nothing but the best for her that we can provide."

Emmeric stood and wrapped his arms around Rose.

♥

Fiona's stomach rumbled. *Food.* Her eyes shifted to the tray. "What's the worst that can happen?" It could be poisoned. She laughed. "Maybe a handsome prince will save me. Fiona, the only one saving your sorry butt is you." She studied her breakfast: boiled eggs, toast, and orange juice. *Still warm. Someone was just in my room. Pushy or someone else.* She trembled. "Should I even eat this stuff?" She nervously carried the tray to a table, by the window, removed a dust cover from a wing back chair and opened the shutters before sitting. Morning light brightened the dark room. She took one last look at the food. She sighed. Took a sip. Took a bite. She was still okay. In a matter of minutes the food was gone. She looked at her hands. "I haven't been poisoned. I'm still here."

Fiona viewed another courtyard from her room. Not the main one with the fountain. The cobbles were wet from last night's rain. She spotted Gilly and Lorcan playing and another horse she hadn't seen before. *I bet that's a mare. She has a real pretty face. I wonder if that's Lorcan's mother?* She knocked on the window to get Gilly's attention. Gilly looked up and whinnied and flicked her tail. *She seems okay.* "I wonder how Tess, Tilda and the sheep are managing."

Knock. Knock.

Fiona jumped up from the chair. "Hello?"

"Are you okay in there?" It was Pushy.

"Why don't you come in and find out for yourself." She looked around for a weapon.

Silence.

"Did you hear me?" Fiona listened at the door.

Silence.

Fiona was frustrated. "Come back." She turned and walked away, kicking at the rug.

Fiona set about exploring her room. She found an old fashioned water pitcher and wash basin, soap and towels. Next to it was a beautiful tortoise shell and boar bristle brush and comb set. A mirror was attached to the dresser. *This stuff is old but in good shape.* She washed up and brushed out her ratty hair, pulling it back with a band. "That's better."

She opened dresser drawers. Old lace camisoles and pretty handkerchiefs were neatly folded in the top drawer. The bottom drawer was stiff, but she worked it back and forth. It squeaked open. Fancy ladies riding gloves and button down blouses in beautiful fabrics looked brand new. *How was this possible?* She pushed her hands further into the drawer, felt a box, and pulled it out. It was made of wood. A Memory Box, with fancy mother of pearl inlay on the top. *This is strange. How common are Memory Boxes?* "This is beautiful." A red ribbon escaped one edge of the box. She lifted the lid slowly and found a collection of fancy ribbons, unlike anything she'd ever seen, in neat curls: red, yellow, pink, green, and blue. And fancy dress buttons from ages ago. And an ivory chess piece, the Queen. *These must have meant something special to someone.* She carefully placed the box back in the drawer. *I'll never see my Memory Box again, what little I had in it.*

She spotted her duffle peeking out from under the bed and pulled it out. *How come I didn't hear him this close?* She rummaged through it and pulled out a clean change of clothes. *Where's the toilet?* None. Fiona found a porcelain chamber pot and toilet paper under the bed too. "Really? This is barbaric." She moved the pot to a spot in the room hidden from the keyhole in the door. *I don't want Pushy or anyone else peeping.* She never got the chance to try it out.

Knock. Knock.

"Are you decent?" Pushy asked.

Fiona jumped. "You need to stop doing that."

He snickered. "It's my job."

"Find a different line of work, like helping me to escape."

"I can't do that," Pushy said.

"Please, please." She wasn't afraid of Pushy.

No answer.

She didn't have a bad feeling about him in her gut, like with Magnus and Ronan. *He's not in charge. Maybe he's a prisoner too.*

No answer. She flopped back in the wing back chair; brow furrowed and stared out the window.

Dangerous Devices

The crowing woke Gilly and the others in the stables. *I wonder if Fiona heard them?* Gilly raised herself up and shook the fresh straw off. She yawned even though she wasn't tired. She forgot where she was for a moment. The sound of big horses snorting and whinnying brought her back to reality. *Not at Quimby Farm.* "Fiona! Tess! Tilda! Where are you?" She shook off the remaining sleep, now wide awake.

Brora peeked her head in to check on the new arrival. "How did you sleep, pretty girl?"

Gilly startled. "Oh, Brora...fine. But where is everyone?"

"You must mean your traveling companions." Brora smiled. "They're fine, I'm sure. They must be awake by now. The dogs and sheep are in their stalls."

"Can't they come out?"

"It's up to Magnus. Not to worry. He knows what's best for everyone," Brora said. "Besides, you've got Lorcan to play with."

Joy! Not. Gilly decided she'd better play along and keep Brora happy. She wasn't so bad anyway. "Great!"

"You two can play after the boy feeds us," Brora said.

"Can I at least see my friends?" Gilly tilted her head down and pawed the ground.

"That's up to Magnus or Ronan."

Lorcan showed up before Gilly finished her breakfast. "Hey. You ready, slowpoke?"

Head down in the hay, Gilly rolled her eyes. "I didn't realize that we were having an eating contest. Guess you beat me again." *I'll get you, you arrogant colt!* In her sweetest voice she said, "Can we check on the dogs and sheep? Oh, maybe you'd better ask first…to see if it's okay."

"Hmpff!" Lorcan puffed out his chest. "I can make that decision, no problem. I don't need to ask anyone. Come on."

Gilly followed behind Lorcan, making faces at him, as they wove their way through the maze of corridors. The clop-clop sounds echoed off the dark stone walls. *I wonder if Tess and Tilda can tell that it's me heading their way.* They rounded a corner.

"Hey, where are you two going?" one of the sentry horses said. "Get out of here."

Lorcan puffed out his chest. "I'm showing our guest…"

"Not here, you're not. Strict orders from your father." The sentry pinned his ears back and bared his teeth.

Lorcan reared up and squealed in a tantrum before galloping away. Gilly was fast on his hooves, afraid of what the big sentry horse might do to her. They bolted through the stables labyrinth, arriving at the big tree away from the castle, the one they had raced to yesterday. Winded, they huffed and blew air out in loud snorts.

As…I…thought. A…chicken…livered… Gilly tried to catch her breath, *spoiled…brat.* "Lorcan, you're so brave. You told him! Thanks for saving me from the fierce sentry…" *That you ran from.*

Lorcan flashed a smile and strutted around Gilly. "I am brave." He was too winded to puff out his chest.

"Lorcan! Gilly! Are you two behaving?" Brora called out from the stables. "Come play in the courtyard."

Gilly turned her head towards Brora's voice.

Lorcan rolled his eyes. "Yes, Mother."

They were breathing hard and puffing after escaping the sentry. *No doubt we were close to where the dogs and sheep are being held. If I can remember how to get back there. I need to see Fiona to tell her.* She looked up from

the courtyard, in time to see Fiona throw open shutters on a window in the tower section. Gilly let out a
deep breath, and whinnied, thrilled at seeing Fiona. She
flicked her tail. Fiona waved and smiled. *She's okay!* Gilly
ran after Lorcan in a game of tag.

"Lorcan, what's behind all those doors?" Gilly
pointed her muzzle.

"Old stuff, from when the humans lived here, a long
time ago."

"Can we go see?"

"Well, I'm not allow—," Lorcan said.

"Pl-ease."

I wonder why he's not supposed to go there. Gilly was
no stranger to getting into trouble and she could convince the show-off to break the rules.

"Follow me," Lorcan said. He looked around, making
sure the coast was clear. "This is really cool." He pawed
the ground. "But dangerous."

They approached a series of archways, hugging the
stone wall and remaining in the shadows as they walked.
Some wood doors were intact and closed. Others splin-
tered and broken. Lorcan unexpectedly ducked into one
of the open doorways. Gilly followed him into the darkness. It took time for her eyes to adjust. It was cooler
here than in the sunny courtyard. It smelled damp and
musty, like rotted fabric and leather. She turned up her

upper lip, and raised her head, at the stink. It didn't seem to bother Lorcan.

Eyes adjusted, Gilly squealed in delight.

"Lorcan, you're right. Wow! Carts and wagons."

"See, I told you, this is neat stuff." Lorcan snapped his head, acting as if he'd been there a hundred times. He stepped in front of her. "Don't touch, Gilly. You could get hurt!"

"Don't be silly." Gilly pushed past him and whinnied a laugh. "We have these where I come from. But you've got fancy ones too, that I've never seen before." She stepped gingerly over cart shafts and smelled each one. She sneezed. There were rows and rows of them. The once bright colors were covered in decades of dust. "Why shouldn't they be touched?"

Lorcan gave Gilly a horrified look. "Stories have been passed down for generations, how these were used by the humans to enslave us. A number of my ancestors have been killed by humans after one of these devices crashed into us or falls onto us."

"Nonsense. It's who we are. It's what we live for. And I can't wait till I'm old enough to pull one," Gilly said.

Lorcan snorted. "Not here, you won't. Magnus and Ronan forbid controlling devices of human origin. That's why your h-halter was removed."

"It's a partnership, Lorcan. We work together with

the humans and in return they take care of us. These are 'implements of transportation.' I bet some of these would be fun in a race." Gilly nudged one of the big wheels.

Lorcan gasped.

"See, nothing bad happened." Gilly smiled at Lorcan and batted her long blonde eyelashes. "Try it." She pushed him closer to a cart.

His head went up and eyes widened. "No, no, I couldn't."

"Show me how brave you are."

Lorcan touched the wheel with his muzzle and took a step back. He breathed a sigh. He tried it again and then smiled.

Gilly urged him to walk deeper in the room. They went single file, gently tip-hoofing over the shafts that lay along the floor like tree limbs. She encouraged him to touch and explore everything. "Can't you just imagine pulling one of these, cleaned up of course, the wind blowing your mane as you trot your finest trot? Showing off for all to see, especially Magnus and Ronan. Imagine how jealous the others would be at what you'd accomplished. You would be in control over the device."

Lorcan turned. "Yeah, yeah. I'd be braver and better than Ronan. Magnus will make me second in command over everyone! I can call the shots over the sentry horses."

"Fiona can show you how safe they are."

Lorcan shook his head and snorted. "No… it's not right. We better get out of here." He gave Gilly a look. "Besides, why would I trust your human?"

Because you're vain and won't admit defeat. Gilly nickered.

shadow

He stood outside her door and listened. Nothing. Rapped on the solid door. Knock. Knock. Knock. She yelped and he smiled to himself.

"What do you want?" Fiona said.

He peeked through the old keyhole in the door. She stood near the window. Interrupted, he supposed, from looking down at the courtyard. Now moving toward the door. Wood floors creaking.

"I said, what do you want? You keep knocking at the door, but obviously you don't have the guts to come in— unless I'm asleep."

He growled, "Magnus wants to see you." He quickly unlocked and cracked open the door, throwing a fabric hood in before she could reach him. "Put that on and turn around." He spied through the keyhole to make sure that she had complied.

"Good morning to you, too, Pushy," Fiona said in a snarky voice.

He'd hoped she'd be no trouble. Then he assessed the situation before entering the room. She wasn't standing next to anything and her hands appeared to be empty. But he could see that she was angry, hands fisted at her side. He took a deep breath before entering the room. "Stay where you are." He grabbed her arms, but she pulled free, ripped the hood off, and swung the hood and slammed a balled fist into his face.

He stumbled backwards, catching himself before he fell. "What the—"

Fiona ran full force into him, spilling them both to the floor. He found himself in a tangle of hair, arms and legs, they rolled and kicked around. He scissored his legs around hers. She pounded on his head. He pinned her arms to her sides with his own.

"Get off of me boy. Get off of me, you moron!" Fiona shouted.

"Calm down, will ya? You're not doing either of us any good," he hissed.

"What the hell? Let me go."

"Not till you calm down," he said. "What's with the Pushy bit?"

"Well, you are! Ordering me around and spying on

me. What gives? What's with the horses? This is crazy! Get off of me!"

"As soon as you calm down and act normal." He kept his arms pressed around her.

"How would you know what's normal? You live with these horses and take orders from them!"

"Look at me! Don't you know who I am?"

Fiona stopped struggling and looked into his eyes. Her gaze locked with his. He saw that she was lost in the depths of them. He waited for signs of recognition from her. Her breathing slowed down. "You. You're…" She went rigid and then limp. He untangled himself from her and knelt over her.

"Fiona?"

Fiona was in her bedroom. The new house in Agawam Point. The big flowers on the old torn wallpaper turned orange then crumpled brown as the flames licked up the walls. No way out. A dark towering shadow approached.

"What do you want?" she asked nervously. The flames, always the flames.

A boy's voice answered. Not a bogey-man. "Fiona, we need to get out of here. Hurry!"

Flames licked up the walls behind the boy-shadow.

He knows my name. Who is he?

The smoke curled into the bedroom. It thickened, and she coughed, wrenching her stomach. Her throat tightened. She backed up to the window and felt the fresh air behind her. There was no good way to escape from the boy-shadow or the flames. Just the window.

The boy coughed in fits and pushed against her. "Jump! Jump!"

He kept pushing. She felt her body squeezed through the window. Like being folded in half. Felt the fresh air. His face so close. I know that voice.

Pushy! Always pushing. But not Pushy. His face came into view. Green eyes, freckles, red hair. It was like looking in a mirror.

FINN!

Felt the ground and the pain. Then felt nothing.

She heard Finn say, "It's all my fault." He was close to her on the ground. "I have to go away..."

BROTHER!

♥

"Are you okay? Did I hurt you…?"

Fiona recalled the ceiling fan in her room at the farm. It had four blades. Finn represented the fourth blade, the one she could never remember. She came from a family of four.

"Finn?" Fiona asked slowly. She opened her eyes and

looked at him. Recognition dawned. She reached for his hair. "I figured it out. The shadow—it was you the whole time. You saved me. You weren't trying to kill me, were you?"

Finn sat back on the floor and put his hands to his face. "I killed Mom and Dad. I almost killed you." He cried.

Fiona caught her breath, and sat up, and tentatively put her hand on Finn's shoulder. "Please, tell me it was an accident. In my vision I heard you say you 'had to go away.' Why?"

"I couldn't live with myself, Fi."

"But it was an accident!" She pulled away. "Wasn't it?"

"Yes." Finn sobbed. "I hate myself." Tears flowed down his cheeks.

Fiona wrapped her arms around her brother and smiled. *I can't believe how big he got. Look at his hair. It's longer than mine.* She held on tight.

"I found out you were okay. I followed the news of your recovery. I found your Facebook page. I hitchhiked across Massachusetts to be near you and found this place. I know it's a ways away."

"What is this place?"

He shrugged. "I call it the Castle."

"How close are we to Fairfield?" Fiona said.

"Not really sure. I got sort of lost exploring. I know we're in Vermont. There's a town not to…"

"Boy! Boy! Bring the girl to me. Now!"

"It's Magnus. Fiona, listen to me." Finn shook Fiona by the shoulders and looked her in the eyes. "Let me answer his questions. And whatever you do, don't let him know that we're brother and sister." Finn wiped his wet face and dripping nose on his shirt sleeve. He handed her the hood.

"Why not?" Fiona asked.

"It would mean death to one of us and I'm pretty sure the one dying would be you."

"Why me?"

Finn looked down at the floor, embarrassed. "Because you're a girl."

Fiona gasped.

"Put the hood on and behave. Don't be snappy with him."

They wound their way down the stairs. Finn told her when to step down. He had a firm hold of her arms.

"Try not to push," Fiona said.

Rules

A commotion of hooves and whinnies came from the main courtyard. "Let's see what's going on," Gilly said. "There's your dad. What's he going to do with Fiona and the boy?"

"Make sure you stay out of the way," Lorcan said.

They raced through several archways and came to an abrupt halt at the edge of one, in time to see Fiona and the boy emerge from the front door of the castle into the early morning light. Gilly and Lorcan pushed and shoved each other to get the best vantage point. Lorcan, being bigger, won. Gilly skootched her head under his, craning her neck forward. Magnus and Ronan stood with their backs to Gilly and Lorcan. They faced the two human children. Magnus flicked his tail. Gilly gasped at seeing the cloth hood over Fiona's head.

The boy leaned into Fiona. His lips moved. She couldn't make out what he said.

"Remove the hood," Magnus commanded.

Fiona pulled the hood off. Red hair tumbled in her face. Magnus took a step back. His head went up in the air. Gilly knew that Magnus was surprised. Gilly focused on Fiona and the boy to see why Magnus was surprised. And stepped back into Lorcan.

"Hey watch it," he said.

She remained still. Obviously, Magnus had seen the red hair too. *Why hadn't Magnus reacted the day we arrived?* The boy and Fiona looked almost identical. The boy was taller and his red hair was longer than Fiona's. And scraggly. It covered his human ears and flopped over his eyes and down to his shoulders. *Emmeric never had hair that long. Only girls have long hair.*

Gilly snickered, "It looks like a Haflinger mane."

Lorcan bumped her. "Shhh."

She nodded.

Magnus stepped forward and sniffed the humans. "You carry the same horrible human scent." He snorted. "Are you of the same family?"

The boy answered, giving Fiona a kick at the same time. "No, Magnus." He looked at Fiona. He appeared nervous and stuttered. "W—we are from—the same—t—town."

Magnus shook his head. He shook his mane. "You wouldn't lie to me, Finn?"

"N—no, Magnus." He sounded sincere under all that hair. Fiona shot the boy a look, then looked at the ground.

Magnus had to have noticed the look. Fiona was hiding something.

"Girl, what say you?" Magnus grumbled.

"It's true. We're from the same town," she said softly.

Gilly never heard Fiona speak so humbly. She was always outspoken. *Maybe that was some of the details that she couldn't remember.*

"I couldn't remember. I had an accident…I've had trouble with my memory. Uh, Finn helped me remember," Fiona admitted.

Magnus took on a more relaxed stance. "What name do you go by, girl?"

"Fiona."

"Fiona?" Magnus whinnied a laugh. "And you expect me to believe that you two are not related?" He spun around and reared up. His hooves just missed hitting them. "His given name is Finn and yours is Fiona. Do you take me for a fool? Do you all have red hair and names beginning with F? You humans always had a strange way of assigning names. Even when humans ruled us, but that will never happen again…Stories have been handed down, your system of naming…Ach!"

"Yikes!" Gilly backed into Lorcan.

"Hush up, Gilly. You'll give us away," Lorcan said.

Ronan turned toward the noise by the archway. "You two, out you come."

Gilly approached the horses and children. She tried to catch Fiona's eye. Lorcan followed stepping on her hind hooves. "Ow."

"Stand here quietly, unless asked to speak. Understood?" Ronan shot them a look.

Magnus snorted. "Lorcan, stay by my side. Watch and learn. You will be in charge one day, my son. Little Gilly, you are welcome here." Magnus returned his attention to Finn and Fiona.

Gilly and Lorcan nodded.

Fiona sighed. "I told you the truth. We're from the same town. No direct relation, though. Distant cousins, perhaps." She looked at Finn and Gilly. "Most of us have red hair and names beginning with F, except for those who marry into our town-line…" She looked at Gilly. "…the way Haflingers are named and look and…"

Was Fiona telling the truth? If not, this is a great performance. I can usually tell when Fiona tells a long tale to Emmeric. Her head is down, and I can't see her eyes…

Magnus snorted. "You're giving me a headache. Quiet!"

Hmmm, Magnus gets impatient with long explanations. I'll make sure that Fiona knows this. Maybe it will come in handy...

Fiona looked up. Her eyes connected to Gilly's. Gilly pawed the ground. Fiona smiled back.

"Here are the rules," Magnus announced to Fiona. "You will remain here. You will serve the boy as well as me and my herd. Try to escape, you will be killed. If one of the animals you brought tries to escape, the same fate awaits. Gilly has free run of the estate—but she too must learn her place among us." Magnus turned to Lorcan. "You will make sure of that. Finn will instruct the girl on our routine and hers. Ronan, let loose the dogs and sheep after they've been instructed. Any resistance—kill the offender."

Fiona gasped, and stumbled back.

"Yes, Magnus." Ronan trotted away toward the stables.

"Questions?" Magnus stared hard at Gilly and the humans.

They shook their heads solemnly.

Reunion

Gilly flattened her ears as Magnus yelled at Ronan, "Relieve the night sentries. Charge the day sentries with their orders to patrol the borders." Magnus and Ronan abruptly turned away and sped off at a trot.

The morning dew was heavy. Last night was the coldest night so far. *Good thing we found this place yesterday, and Finn lit a fire in my room.* Fiona's thoughts were interrupted when Ronan, making a dash, slipped on the wet cobblestones. He gathered himself up.

"Yes, Magnus—" His voice faded when they split up, heading in different directions.

Fiona and Finn let out deep breaths. Fiona shivered even though she was wearing a sweatshirt. Without his father around, Lorcan assumed a relaxed posture, rear hoof tipped.

"Where are those two going?" Fiona asked.

Finn glanced nervously in Lorcan's direction. "I'll explain everything on the tour." He stomped his foot and glared, "Beat it you two! Go eat some hay or something."

Gilly stepped back, eyes wide.

"Don't yell at her!" Fiona went to Gilly and stroked her. "I know he upset you, girl. But it's okay."

Gilly nudged at Fiona. The filly trudged away, and Lorcan followed.

She put her hands on her hips and narrowed her eyes. "I don't treat my horses that way. Don't ever yell at her!"

"Sorry," Finn said. "Come on, I'll show you around." He motioned for her to walk.

They moved from the sunny courtyard to an archway, where they were met with cooler air in the shadows. Fiona let out a deep breath and looked at Finn through her visible breath. She shivered. *Where do I begin?*

She opened her mouth and the words fell out. "What's up with you? When did you start being so mean?" *I don't know, maybe he was...* There were lots of missing pieces to the puzzle that was her family. She hated puzzles. Could she trust her own brother? Her parents were dead, and he'd left her alone, lying on the ground unconscious.

All he said was, "Sorry, stress from Magnus and Ronan. They're hard to deal with."

"Stressed or not, I try not to talk to Gilly like that. She's my friend."

"Guess it's been awhile since I've had a friend." He smiled.

Finn led her to the kitchen. It was large compared to Rose's cozy farmhouse kitchen. The wood countertops were old, well-worn and gouged-out from years of butchering. Rickety cabinets hung along two walls. Dishes and glasses were scattered on the countertop. *Housekeeping is not his forte!* She spotted a couple of fancy tea cups, reminding her of the one that had been in her Memory Box back at the farm. "Primitive."

"But it works. No fancy cooking here," he replied.

"That explains the smoke we saw." Fiona pointed to the fireplace. "Looks like a witch's cauldron hanging there. You go grocery shopping? Where? I didn't exactly spot a Whole Foods store." She shrugged her shoulders. "Where's the fridge? I don't get it."

He chuckled. "I get by. But don't ask too many questions. Listen, Fi, sorry again. Magnus and Ronan make me jumpy. I didn't mean to yell at your horse, but I didn't want to talk in front of Lorcan."

"Fine. I get it. Is there *anyone* you can trust?"

"Maybe Brora. Lorcan's mother."

"Oh, the pretty one. I saw her out of the window from my room."

They walked into a massive library. Fiona stopped and looked at the massive wall-to-ceiling collection of books. Mouth gaped open. She spun around in a circle. *A lifetime of reading! Impressive…but this place, the nasty horses.* She closed her eyes and mind from the books. Her mind snapped back to Finn. She grabbed his arm. "Why did you stay here? I don't get it."

He strained a laugh and shrugged. "Where would I go? Who wants to adopt a criminal? They'd just put me in jail. I'm serving my sentence here—where I belong."

She looked deep into his eyes. "What happened?"

"I didn't want to move, remember?"

She grabbed his arms, hard. "Finn, *did* you set the fire on purpose?"

"I was mad at Mom and Dad."

She spoke slowly. "Was it on purpose?"

"No! I went down in the basement looking for my airplane model. I wanted to get it unpacked and make sure nothing broke from the move. I don't know…there was some smelly stuff around in old cans. Like turpentine or something. And piles of junk from the old owners. I—I was using my lighter to find a light switch—and—I don't know—it just—it just—happened. Whoosh! I was knocked on my butt and scrambled to get upstairs. The flames followed me up. I couldn't think—I didn't know what to do." He sniffled.

"The lighter? You still had the damn lighter? Mom made you get rid of it," she yelled.

"I—I had another one," he admitted.

Fiona sunk into a chair. "Oh, Finn. Oh, Finn. It was a stupid accident." She sobbed.

Finn was quiet.

Fiona felt his eyes on her.

"I r—ran to your room first…I—I didn't have time to g—get to Mom and Dad."

"The shadow—you—you *pushed me!*" Fiona shuddered.

"I *saved* you! You know that now? How can I convince you?"

She wiped her face and sniffled. "We'll go to the police and get it straightened out. You can leave this place and come live with us." *Emmeric always wanted a boy. I don't know if they'd want him, after what he did.* She gave him a sideways glance. *Would they keep him and replace me, after what I've done? I shouldn't promise anything.*

"I can't," Finn said.

"Well, maybe in a while, after it's all investigated and figured out," she said.

"No, I mean, I have to take care of this place and the horses."

"*They* can take care of themselves." Fiona was angry and raised her voice.

Finn frowned and shook his head. "You don't understand. I can't leave here.

And neither can you!"

Reunion 2

"The horses don't want to be found," Finn said.

"We're prisoners. Forever?" Fiona was quiet, thinking. "If we work together—"

"Fiona, you don't get it. No one leaves here alive!"

"How do you know that? Do you even want to escape?" Fiona felt waves crashing in the pit of her stomach.

He gave a lopsided smile and looked away.

Why won't he answer me? I am officially freaked out. I don't think I can count on him for any help.

Finn continued the tour. Fiona followed dutifully. She felt numb and his talking rambled on like background noise. She didn't hear what he was saying. It didn't sink in. *I may as well have died with Mom and Dad.* She ran away from Finn, through the castle, warm tears on her cheeks. "Air. I need air," she screamed.

She felt dizzy. She found herself in yet another court-yard and plopped down on a stone wall. Barking and bleating sounds found their way through the muddle in her mind. Girl's voices came closer. *Methra, I think, saying she hopes I'm unharmed.* This snapped her out of her funk. She saw them—her true friends. She could barely get the names out: "Tess, Tilda, Yan, Tan, Tethera, Methra." Fiona held her arms open and fell to her knees. "I've missed you all so much." Slobber and paws-hooves and fur-wool covered her. Dog and sheep tongues fought for space on her face. She laughed and rolled on the ground.

Finn came into the courtyard. "Here you are. I was looking for you. Why'd you run off?"

"You probably wouldn't understand," Fiona said and shot him an angry look.

"Hey listen Fi, have fun with your animals and don't wander off."

"Why, where are you going?"

"I have some errands to run."

"Magnus and Ronan let you do that?" She sounded shocked. "They trust you?"

"Don't even think about following me." He smirked. "Stay with your pets, and be a good girl."

A growl rose up from Tess, her hackles raised. "Easy, girl." Fiona petted her.

"Oh, and you'll be fixing all the meals from now on. And cleaning. There's no mom here to do it for you." He turned to walk away.

Boy, did his mood turn. *Yeah, well you took care of that. Didn't you?* She scowled and made faces at his back.

Finn out of sight, she got up off the ground and brushed herself off. "Let's look for Gilly."

"She's probably with the colt," Tess said. "Is Finn your brother?"

Fiona hesitated. "He's not acting like my brother. The horses have him brainwashed." Fiona looked down at Tess. "We can't trust him. At least not right now. Don't let on to Magnus and Ronan that we're brother and sister. I think they feel a boy human is worth more to them than a girl human. If any of us try to escape they'll kill us!" *I hope he comes around. I don't want to lose him again.*

Fiona cupped her hands and yelled, "Gilly! Gilly!"

She heard a whinny in the distance. She hollered, "Come on, girl. Your friends are here."

Gilly galloped through one of the archways and slid to a stop on the cobblestones. She reared up and gave a huge whinny. Her tail flicked, and she pawed the stones. "Where have you all been? Lorcan and I are having a great time. I love this place."

Fiona's mouth dropped open. "About that, we need to talk—"

Tess pulled at her pants. "Maybe later, Fi."

She looked into Tess's eyes. "Y—you're right. It can wait, Gilly." She cleared her throat and looked around. "Where is Lorcan? What have you and he been doing?"

"I left him grazing. He doesn't care. We've been playing and exploring. He's a pain, but he's mostly fun," Gilly said. "I met his mom, Brora. She's really nice. And I have a great stall with lots of straw…"

"Okay, girl. I get it." She smiled and rubbed Gilly's ears and muzzle.

"Fiona, I want to show you the carts and wagons we found. This way," Gilly said. "Emmeric has some carts like these. Wait until you see."

They all followed. *Field trip,* Fiona thought to herself.

The sound of hooves and feet and paws echoed on the cobbles. Wary, Fiona listened for the other horses. Nothing. *Finn doing 'errands' and the nasty horses are doing who knows what. Brora is still a mystery…* She relaxed and let out a deep breath. *May as well try to figure this place out and see what Gilly's discovered.*

Gilly led them through an arched doorway. Fiona stopped dead in her tracks. "This is incredible. I've never seen so many carts and wagons." She hurried up and down the aisles managing not to trip over the shafts. There was so much to see, even under the thick coating of dust. Incredible colors: blue, green, red and black.

Gold pin striping: lines and curlicues. A wheel leaning next to a cart caught her foot, and she stumbled. "Argh."

"Careful," Tess said.

Fiona, jogging, turned to thank Tess and came to an abrupt stop, into the side of a large green wagon. "Ow." She rubbed her shoulder.

Her friends all laughed. Fiona laughed and shook her head too at her clumsiness. She felt relief. "I think I'll walk my way around the rest of the room." She found an old rag and wiped off an area of dust on the side of the green wagon. "This is beautiful." Her eyes followed the gold curlicues. "How did all of this get here? Why did the owners leave the castle? I wonder if any of the horses know?"

After some time, Fiona noticed that she and Tess were the only ones left in the Carriage House. Her stomach rumbled. *Must be around lunch time.* "I guess everyone got bored. The sheep are probably grazing, and Tilda and Gilly are napping under a big tree somewhere. Let's go check out what there is to eat."

Fiona relaxed her strides and breathed in the fresh air—no Finn, no horses. Tess wagged her tail and circled Fiona nipping at her heels. "May as well make myself to home. Right, girl?"

Tess smiled.

"After all, if I'm spending the rest of my life here..." Fiona tripped on a cobble.

They wound their way through the maze of archways off of the main courtyard. They entered the castle and explored despite a rumbling stomach. The rooms went on and on. No sooner did Fiona find a new room then she found herself back in a room she'd already been in. *This is confusing.* "Good, the kitchen," Fiona announced to Tess. "Let's see..." She opened the cabinets and drawers. "Hmm, Fruit Loops, Captain Crunch, Ronzoni, Skippy..." She took a step back and opened her mouth. "How'd Finn pull this off? He can't have any money. Tess, did you spot the cold stuff?"

She pawed at a door, "Look in here, Fi."

Fiona opened the door. A cold earthy smell smacked her in the face. "Whoa." She peered into the darkness. "I need a light, Tess."

Tess ran to a table and grabbed a lantern from it. She ran back for the box of matches. "Here."

"Thanks." Fiona struck a match and lit the lantern. She held it into the darkness. Steps, down.

"Careful," Tess said.

Fiona walked into the earthy cold, down the uneven steps. She swung the lamp in a gentle arc. "It's a storage cellar. Okay, I see milk, eggs. Some cheese, I think. That's weird, why would you put bread down here? Potatoes, onions. Dead animals hanging, obviously killed by Finn. I'm used to this now, thanks to you Tess. I'm coming up."

She emerged with bread and cheese, brushing cobwebs off her arms. "There has to be a town around here somewhere. I'll have to work on gaining Finn's trust and un-brainwashing him." They ate in silence.

"This would have been the place of my dreams for Gilly. But it's just not realistic. I can't live like this. It's too primitive. No electricity, plumbing, or real heat. I'd have to steal or hunt for our food. Gilly would be better off with another farm family. I have no dog food for you or Tilda." She looked at Tess. "I'm so sorry about all of this. I've put everyone in danger. I'm sure Rose and Emmeric are torn up and have had all sorts of police agencies out looking for us. I refuse to be a slave to my brother and the nasty horses." Fiona sighed.

Tess Hightails It

Tess stared at Fiona while she napped—tossing and turning. Her poor friend and mistress mumbled something that didn't even sound like human talk. Her face was contorted and had a look of pain. It must be a dream. Not a pleasant one, like a vet's visit and a long needle. *Do humans have dream terrors? Maybe I should wake her.*

But Tess had already formulated a plan as soon as Fiona proclaimed that a nap was in order. She slinked off the bed onto the floor, barely moving the mattress. She looked back at her friend and felt bad that she would be leaving her in whatever state she was experiencing. Finn had about a three hour lead and she was determined to find out where he had gone off—to do "errands" *I'm no hound. But I have a great sniffer!*

She tip-pawed to the door. Challenge one. A round

knob. Not good. She sat in front of the door, concentrating, trying to block out the sounds of Fiona groaning. It took a number of attempts—paws, teeth, paws and teeth…finally. The knob turned and the door cracked open. Air traveled through the gap. She pushed the door open with her nose, just wide enough to squeeze her body through.

Challenge two. *I need to find where Finn sleeps. I need something with his smell.* She had her nose in the air, ran to several doors. She bent and sniffed the air at the bottom of the doors. Stale, dusty—a sneeze. She ran down the stone steps and through several large rooms, then up another set of winding steps, deciding on the second floor. The air here changed. There were different odors along the long hallway. She spied peeling paint along the walls. An old musty rug covered the length of the hall. Her nose picked up the scent of the outdoors: dirt, grass, hay. Finn had to have walked here. She sniffed under several doors. Ah! A door was cracked open. Her nose pushed it open to reveal a large bed covered in blankets, unmade. Socks on the ground, underwear, shirts and pants in piles. A stack of yellowing newspapers were on a table. A dusty mirror over a dresser had a couple of newspaper clippings shoved between the glass and wood trim. "Hmm." Tess put her paws on the furniture for a closer look.

Early edition

Devastating House Fire Kills Family New to Seaside Community

Child survives. ...suspicious blaze engulfs residence killing parents, leaving girl in critical condition. It is unknown at this time how the girl escaped the blaze... in what has been called a flash fire. Fire fighters still on scene. ... looking for a fourth person, boy living in the home... cause is under investigation. Fire Investigators ask anyone with information to call...

"Finn!"

Tess stopped reading.

Tess rooted through the piles of clothing with her nose. She inhaled slowly and deeply to take in his aromas. Much stronger than Fiona's. She placed the teen-boy-aromas deep in her mind. In a place reserved for *him*, the brother of her beloved Fiona.

Challenge three. Getting past the horses. She lost no time in bounding down the steps and out of the house into the daylight. She couldn't risk Fiona waking right now to look for her. Fiona would have to be kept out of this. Tilda, as young as she was, would still keep an eye on Fiona.

Tess perked her ears for the sounds of horses and sheep. If they discovered her it would spell the end of finding where Finn had gone. The sun was high in the sky signaling mid-day. Everyone would be lazy by now. But she didn't know the habits of the "nasty horses", as Fiona called them, and couldn't predict where they might be.

She slinked low to the ground as if rounding up sheep. Ran to the main archway, past the fountain. She'd need to catch an old scent of Finn's to determine which way to go. Nose in the air, she moved her nostrils, catching a breeze. Nose to the ground, she scanned back and forth for a scent. There it was. Very faint. She slinked in a low crawl. The grasses were tall and made for good cover. She stopped and listened. Horses snorted in the distance. She spotted a path of sorts and broken grasses. She sniffed Finn's smell. Trees in the distance. She bolted for cover. Safe, so far.

Her nose caught the breeze and then the ground. She gathered herself up and followed the path through the woods. Ears twitched. A horse snorted, closer this time. She bolted as fast as she could go along the path. Snorting faded. She was panting and would have to get that under control. She scanned the dirt and leaves of the forest floor. She found an impression of a human shoe and studied it. She gently inhaled from the impression. *It's him and I can see the direction he's taking. Now, to make up time and catch up.* Tess hightailed it.

Her ears perked up. She heard sounds that she hadn't

heard since leaving the farm—trucks and cars. She'd have to cross a road. Cautiously, she emerged from the woods. She knew the danger of crossing roads. She had been warned countless times as a pup and had even seen the results of careless crossings in the form of squashed cats and lame dogs. Even though Quimby Farm was on a gravel lane the humans came speeding by, kicking up dust and rock, no caution given to animals. A deadly game of tag. She had her paws full when Tilda was a pup. Tilda thought it great fun to herd tires. Thankfully, she grew out of that obsession intact.

Tess studied the pace and speed of the cars. They whizzed by at an incredible speed. This was no country lane. This was a busy road. The trucks made a horrible noise when they passed, almost sucking her out of her hiding spot. There was no other way to track Finn. She had to cross and stay on his scent.

She drew in a breath, studied a break in the traffic and ran for it. She made it to the double line but something wasn't right. Another truck swung out from behind the truck that she'd spotted. Two trucks were heading for her side-by-side. One was to the right of the double line, the other to the left. There was no time to go back. Air horns blared. She was so confused. Stay, run, stay, run? She hunkered down on the lines and closed her eyes, praying that this was not the end. She felt the whoosh on both sides of her as the huge trucks passed. The horns were deafening.

She opened her eyes to see that another truck was bearing down. In a daze, she bolted for the shoulder of the road. She didn't know if she made it across or if in all the confusion ran back to the side from which she came. She ran into the woods and collapsed, tongue lolling and panting profusely. *I almost died today…*

Houses came into view. Finn was still nowhere in sight but his scent was stronger. She'd have to sneak past the houses and avoid being seen. Humans did not take kindly to strange dogs roaming through their territories. She had seen Emmeric shoot strays on the farm to keep them away from the lambs and chickens. Many times she and Tilda chased the intruders. Emmeric had trained them to chase strange dogs away to protect the livestock.

Another road. Not so bad. She spotted a cluster of rooftops. They were close together, looking nothing like a farm or human house. *Must be a town of humans: lots of people, roads and…trucks!* A chill ran through her. *Shake it off.*

In the distance a massive gray stone structure rose above the treetops, pointy at the top. Stealthily, she crossed the roads. Bells rang out from another huge stone structure with a number of pointy tops. She ran.

Car horns blared. She found herself in the middle of a road, heart pounding, tail tucked and ears flat— looking around to figure out which way to go. She began panting. *Keep your head on straight. Stay calm.* She ran to a sidewalk and hugged the bushes to stay out of view.

The smell of car and truck exhausts in the air masked Finn's scent. She twitched her nose in the air and sneezed from the fumes. Head down, running, she scanned the sidewalk with her nose. A jumble of scents. She couldn't hone in on Finn.

A boy's voice yelled, "Mommy, Mommy look a doggie." She backed away as the little boy approached, his hand held out to pet her.

"No, Bobby! That's a strange dog. Come back here right this minute!" a woman shrieked.

Tess ran around the corner of a brick building and stopped short, hunkering to the ground. A pair of human feet and legs was pointed up in the air. The body balanced precariously on the edge of a big blue container. She couldn't see the head. Her nose picked up the scent of heaven—garbage. And a good assortment of it. The feet and legs came back down to the ground and a red head popped up out of the bin. Finn. In his hands, boxes and cans similar to what she'd seen in the castle's kitchen. The boy quickly stuffed his catch into a plastic bag and looked around. He scooped up his pack and bags and walked quickly to an alley.

Tess followed at a safe distance. She scanned the area, constantly on guard for humans. She entered the narrow alley once he was through. He stopped at some large green containers by an area of parked cars. He looked around too. Plastic bags were on the ground and overflowed from the container. Quickly, he ripped into the plastic. He looked around again and pulled out some shirts and pants. He held them up and regarded them a piece at a time, and then held the shirts and pants to his body in mere seconds. He stuffed most of the clothes into his backpack. The rest he hastily threw onto the plastic bag that they'd come from. Finn spun around. A car was coming into the parking lot. He ducked behind the containers. When the car drove past he ran through another alley.

Tess's hackles rose. She noticed that a group of human teens had spotted her and were heading her way. *Time to go.* She figured that she'd seen enough to let Fiona know what Finn was doing and what his "errands" were all about. It made sense now, how he was able to survive at the castle.

She crossed the streets, ever aware of the traffic. She spotted a sign that she hadn't noticed before: "Thank you for visiting Bennington." She yipped at the sign, knowing that this was an important tidbit of information for Fiona. Civilization was not all that far away. She left the town and area of houses cutting through a cemetery, or so a sign said, winding her way around standing stones. She wound her way back through the woods at a run. She growled when she finally reached the big road where she had almost died. It was crazy busy. There were too many cars and trucks coming from both directions. She felt dizzy watching. The vehicles whizzed by. She howled. *How will I survive this crossing?* She took in a number of deep breaths and studied the pace of the vehicles. *I have to get across.* She blinked once. Opened her eyes and ran for her life.

She was still in one piece. On the other side of the road.

In the woods. Panting.

Heart-to-Heart

Fiona bolted upright in bed. She grabbed her chest and looked around, confused. The room was dark. "Who's there?" she said, out of breath.

As careful as she was, the bed shook when Tess climbed up. "Fiona, are you okay?" She licked her face.

"I had horrible nightmares. I'm scared."

She laid her paws over Fiona's legs. "You slept all afternoon. It's nighttime."

Fiona pushed off the covers. "Where is everyone?" She jumped out of bed and ran to the window. The courtyard appeared empty. "I'd better check on Gilly and the sheep. Where's Finn? Why is my door open?"

Tess hesitated in answering.

"Well, what's going on?"

"I haven't heard him yet. I don't think he's returned," she said.

"Oh, great. I hope he didn't run out on us, leaving me as his replacement."

"No…he'll be back."

"You know something? Spill the beans, Tess."

"You were sleeping so hard. I decided to see where he was going to do 'errands.'"

"And…" Fiona encouraged.

"Dangerous, dangerous roads to cross. It's several hours away by foot. He goes to a town."

"Really!" Fiona was encouraged.

"It's real. I followed him," Tess said.

Fiona pulled her hair back into a ponytail, throwing her sweatshirt on last. "Come on Tess. Tell me the rest. We'd better check on everyone in the stables."

She jumped from the bed and was next to Fiona in a flash.

"Wait. We need to find a lamp." She looked around the room. "Over there, Tess by the wash basin." She pointed for Tess's benefit.

Tess grabbed the lantern. She was getting good at retrieving.

Fiona reached in her pocket for the box of matches. They left the tower room. And scrambled down the winding steps, lamp held up in front. And flew out the front door into the main courtyard. "Tess, show me where Gilly and the sheep are kept. Tilda's probably with

Gilly." Fiona ran to keep up with her. "Finish telling me while no one else is around."

"Finn was behind buildings, going through metal bins and plastic bags. He found cans and boxes—food and some clothing."

Fiona scrunched up her nose. "Makes sense, with what we've found in the kitchen and cellar."

"One more thing." Tess stopped. "I read a sign that said: 'Thank you for visiting Benneton.' Does that mean anything?"

"Do you mean Bennington?"

"Yeah, that's it."

Fiona dropped to her knees and hugged Tess with all her might. "I know this town. Now I know where we are!"

They ran through archways and corridors. Fiona heard the sounds of bleating, getting closer. *I think one more corner...* "Here you are," Fiona said gasping for air. She leaned against the sheep pen. *Tilda or Gilly must have latched the pen closed. Good thinking.* "Sweet dreams, girls. See you in the morning. Anything you need?"

Yan answered, "Some water if you please, Miss Fiona."

"I have to find the others but I'll be back."

"Tess, which way to Gilly?"

"Follow me."

After a few more turns she navigated another corridor and found herself in the horse section—the stables. She came to a screeching halt. *The nasty horses are probably here, too! I need to avoid them.* She walked on tip-toe, listening intently for horse sounds: snorting, nickering, whinnies, talking. The sound of chewing and clearing nostrils got closer.

"Tess, is there any way to find Gilly and avoid the others?"

"Sure," Tess whispered. "The mares and young ones stay separately from the stallions. This way."

A few more corridors and they found Gilly. "Shush, Gilly girl." Fiona held a finger to her lips. "I don't want to alert Magnus and the sentries."

Gilly nodded her head.

Tilda, lying in Gilly's straw, wagged her tail.

"Are you two okay?" Fiona asked.

Gilly nodded enthusiastically. "Fine, and having a great time. I *love* this place. Is this our new home? Forever?"

"We'll talk tomorrow." Fiona looked around after she spoke. "I hear that there's a mare named Brora."

Mouth full of hay, Gilly flicked her head to the left. "She's over there." It came out mumbled.

"Where's Lorcan?" Fiona asked.

Gilly swallowed. "He stays with the stallions."

"Good," Fiona said.

"What?"

"Never mind. I want to meet Brora. G'night Gilly. You too, Tilda."

Fiona held the lamp in front of her and walked quietly in the direction indicated by Gilly. She raised the lamp up. Light flooded into the stalls as she approached. In one a mare was lying on her straw. Fiona held the lamp over the stall door.

"Sorry to disturb you. Are you Brora?"

The large mare hefted herself up onto her hooves and approached. "Yes, I am. You must be Fiona. I've heard so much about you."

"Thanks, I guess." Fiona stepped back a bit. "You're beautiful, Brora." She reached her free hand forward, and then stopped. "May I pet you?"

"That would be nice." Brora blinked and nickered. "Where's Finn? You two look an awful lot alike."

Fiona shook. "Yeah, that. Uh…we're from the same village. Lots of redheads. Distant cousins, *we* think." *Quick, Fiona, change the subject.* "He's not back from errands. I thought I'd better check on everyone." Fiona looked away from Brora's soft brown eyes.

"He must have gone to town today. He comes back late. I think it's some distance from here."

"Oh?" Fiona didn't let on that she knew.

"He brings back human food. What he can't hunt. And other bits and pieces from your world," Brora said. "He and Magnus have an understanding."

Fiona hung the lamp on a nail and reached for Brora's ears. She breathed gently into Brora's nostrils to further introduce herself. *I do like her!* She smiled and snuggled with the mare who felt relaxed in her arms.

Brora nickered. "I like you, Fiona. Gilly has told me so much about you and your world—a farm where everyone is for sale? Controlled by humans? I just can't imagine a life like that. No offense, but aren't your humans cruel? Quimbys, I believe they are called."

Fiona chuckled. "Actually, no. They *are* really nice humans—my parents, as a matter of fact, the Quimbys." *How do I put this delicately?* "Animals raised on the farm go to good homes with caring people." Fiona gulped on her words, realizing that this was not always true. *Would Brora notice?* She pushed a pebble around with her foot.

"Why did you take Gilly away? If she was to go to a loving home and people?"

"I fell in love with her. I couldn't bear to lose her after losing my parents and Fin—" Fiona's hands flew to her mouth. "Oh, no!"

Brora put her head on Fiona's shoulder. "The truth, Fiona. Always be truthful."

"I'm sorry I lied, Brora. Finn told me that Magnus would kill me if he knew that we were brother and sister."

"That I can believe." Brora lowered her head.

"But why?"

"As brother and sister you cannot be mated. And the boy is more valuable to him than you, I am sorry to say."

Fiona looked horrified. "You won't tell, will you?" Fiona shook.

"I will keep your secret."

She let out a deep breath and wrapped her arms around Brora's neck. The huge mare was soothing to be around.

"Brora, would you know of a horse that may have come from here? A stallion we met along our journey. Rather strange—he loves water."

"Ah, yes, poor thing. He was born of a mare who did not come from here originally. He had a strange proclivity to swim in the creek. He had strange eyes as I remember."

"What happened?" Fiona stroked Brora's side.

"He was to be put to death as a foal, but somehow escaped. His mother, rest her soul, paid with her life for birthing a deformed colt," Brora said.

Fiona gasped. "Well, I can tell you he is alive, but lonely." No point in going into details about their encounter with Kelpinore. She gave Brora a huge hug before leaving.

"Can we talk more tomorrow?" Fiona asked.

"Sure." Brora rubbed her muzzle into Fiona's shoulder. "As long as the stallions are not around, especially Magnus and Ronan and even my little Lorcan."

Fiona thought she felt Brora shudder.

Brother

Fiona, zoned out and tired, headed back to the castle from the stables. She suddenly snapped to and looked around, realizing that she was in the massive library. *How'd I get here?* She remembered Brora's parting words. Goose bumps tingled her skin. *Is it just me, I'm freezing all of a sudden. Nights are getting colder.* She was embroiled in her thoughts, not knowing what to do. Maybe just chance returning to Quimby Farm and face the music—the wrath of Emmeric.

She settled into a comfy chair after lighting the fireplace but couldn't relax. A prickle of discomfort and uncertainty plagued her. Why? She'd accomplished so much: she'd found a castle not a fort, found her brother, found her memory, the animals were relatively safe, but her future seemed as if it had hit a wall. *I could live here with Finn and we could be a family again. I know I can change him, un-brainwash him.* Doubt niggled at her. She shook her head. *What about the 'nasty horses'? Rose says I'm good with animals...I bet with time and work I could bring them around too...* She sighed. Was this all wishful thinking?

She gazed wearily at the bookshelves. *Hmmm, looks like a life-time of reading, my life-time.* She raised her tired body from the chair and scanned the titles. They were all old, "classics." No *Harry Potter* books. She pulled *Kidnapped* from a shelf and blew the dust off the top. She coughed from the swirling powder and sat back down in the chair. The title felt appropriate.

The dogs entered the library snuggling close to the fire. Tilda curled up next to her mother. "Had enough of the barn, Tilda?" Fiona smiled. She didn't make it past page one; her eyes closed. The last thing she heard was a thump on the floor. *Kidnapped.*

Fiona woke to crowing. *Morning already? Where am I?* She stared out the window. *It's so dark. Yuck, rain.* It took her a few seconds to get her bearings and figure out that she'd spent the night in the library. A blanket was tucked up under her chin and around her shoulders. Obviously Finn's doing. The dogs were gone and the remains of the fire smoldered.

She ran up the winding steps to her tower room. On her bed she spied plastic bags. "Clothes. Cool beans!"

She ransacked the bags and held the pants and shirts up. She smelled the jacket before trying it on. "Clean. I knew he wasn't totally brainwashed."

"You call?" Finn stood in the doorway of her bedroom wearing a wry smile.

"Oh, Finn, thanks, thanks." She moved to give him a hug. He backed away. *Go slow with him, Fiona, like you did with Gilly when she was small.* She calmed down. "I really mean it, thanks."

"You never should have come. Don't think you're going to live here like a princess. There's work to do, and now I have to worry about feeding and clothing you too." He pointed to the bed.

"I get that, really. I wasn't looking for *this place*. What do you need me to do?" She bit her lip. She hated taking orders from her older brother. But it had to be done.

"For starters you're in charge of feeding *all* the animals, especially since you brought so many with you. You'll do *all* the cooking and cleaning, like I said before." His brow furrowed. "Especially since I'll have to go off the property more often for supplies. I hope Magnus understands."

Fiona kept her voice low, something Rose taught her to keep animals calm. "Not a problem. I'm just glad we're together again."

"Start now! You missed the morning feedings and

my breakfast." He spun around and clomped down the steps.

She was taken aback by his brusqueness. *Wow, he can be like Emmeric.* She pushed the rising anger down. *I need to understand his stress.* She returned to the bed and picked up her new clothes, putting them away in the dresser. She spied the fancy Memory Box in the bottom drawer and smiled sadly to herself. *I really do love and miss you, Rose.*

Fiona stoked the fire in the kitchen under the hanging black kettle. Even she was surprised how good the rabbit stew smelled—once you got passed the butchering. She tried to push the thought from her mind. *Think vegetables,* she told herself. Finn had a decent supply of onions, potatoes and carrots in the cellar. She'd try to use the staples sparingly.

"I would have fried it, but this smells good," Finn said.

She turned to see him standing in the doorway. His mood had swung the other way. "I hope it's good. I used *our* Mom's stew recipe. Seems you had everything on hand that I needed."

He flashed a quick smile. Sincere this time. Then it was gone. "Don't forget evening feedings and water."

"Sure. I took care of things last night when I saw that

you weren't back, um, ho—. I mean, here." *Will the castle ever feel like home?*

"Thanks."

Sincere again. No defenses this time. Let me try something... "Hey Finn, I noticed that your hair is longer than mine. What would you say to a haircut? I bet it'd feel a lot better." She watched him think for a minute.

"Did you find the scissors?"

"Yea. They're ancient but should work...Have a seat."

She wrapped an old tablecloth around his shoulders. "Hmmm, put your hair in a ponytail." She handed him her band. "I can't give a barber shop cut, but I can get it to above your shoulders."

"That would be fine."

She put her hand on his shoulder and felt him relax. *Good.* She remembered how she used to slide her hand down Gilly's back and under her mane to get her used to human touch and to build trust. "I'll cut off a big clump first, and then try to trim it a bit."

"Just do it."

She felt him stiffen. "Relax. Here goes." It took plenty of muscle for her to get through his thick locks. The scissors were dull from age and use. "Got it." She showed him the ragged ponytail and put it on the table. *I need to build his trust in me.* Her fingers combed through his hair. She snipped here and there to even it out. His shoulders slumped for a brief moment, relaxed.

"Done yet?" He stiffened.

"Yep. You're good to go."

As with young foals, she knew to keep the training sessions short to match their attention span.

"Help! Help!"

"What the..." Finn jumped out of the chair, throwing the tablecloth to the ground.

"Magnus! Ronan!" Shrill whinnies sounded from the courtyard. Hooves clattered on the cobbles.

Fiona grabbed the ponytail from the kitchen table and stuffed it in her pocket. She was fast on Finn's heels as they flew out the kitchen door to the cobbled courtyard out back. "What is it?"

"Lorcan. In a panic," Finn said.

They reached a wide-eyed Lorcan. His nostrils flared and he snorted out his distress. Magnus and Ronan galloped into the courtyard and slid to a stop, just missing Lorcan—dancing around as if a hundred bees had stung him.

Magnus demanded, "What is the meaning of summoning us?"

Out of breath, Lorcan managed an answer. "It's Gilly. She's going to die. The Beast has her!"

Fiona broke in, "What Beast?"

"Follow me." Lorcan spun and headed to one of the arched doorways. Fiona raced on Finn's heals on the slippery, rain-drenched stones.

The Beast

Pinned to the floor amid the fallen pieces of wagons and debris, Gilly heard the ruckus approaching. The clack of hooves and echo of footfalls reverberated off the walls and ceiling of the Carriage House. Fiona and Finn ducked under and jumped over massive wagons, wheels and shafts. Broken bits and pieces of wood and steel lay strewn on the floor. Finn tripped but pulled himself up. Fiona had a more difficult time, stumbling over pieces and landing on her knees. The horses stopped at the door. Gilly knew they couldn't make it through the mess. They were too big. She read the unmistakable sign of terror in their eyes, white and wide. Their ears were laid back and teeth bared as if to threaten the enemy. They puffed and snorted, jigging around. It was too dangerous to venture in among the carriages. Only the humans could free her now.

"Gilly, keep calm. Don't struggle, it will make things worse. Remember the time you got stuck in the fence? We'll get you out," Fiona said.

Finn reached Gilly first. He started to grab at the rubble and pull things out. A wheel fell across her neck. She panicked and tried to pull away. She felt warmth ooze down her neck. *Blood!* A horrible scream left her lips and she struggled more. Things, like teeth, cut into her.

"Finn stop! Gilly, stop! Wait till I get there." Fiona came to Gilly's side and put her soothing hands on her. "Calm, Gilly girl…shush."

She rested her head on the filly's ribs. Gilly's heart raced. "Finn, back away…please. I need to calm her."

Gilly felt Fiona's warmth and love. She relaxed her body and after a time her breathing became normal.

"Finn, we can't just barge in, careful. We need to think this out."

Finn stood up and shrugged. "Whatever. Have you turned into a horse-whisperer or something?"

She brought her head up and shot him a look. "Just the common sense that you're lacking."

Magnus yelled, "What's going on? Is it too late for Gilly?"

Fiona answered, "Some bumps and cuts. I won't know if it's more serious till we get her out."

The humans lifted an axle off a front leg and raised a

wheel, rolling it aside. Piece-by-piece. Next they pulled on her rear legs caught between wheel spokes as if they'd been handcuffed.

"Gilly, what happened?" Fiona asked.

She hesitated, "I wanted to show Lorcan. Make him jealous, that I would pull a fine cart one day and win ribbons and prizes." She nodded her head towards a dust-covered black Meadowbrook cart. "I was trying to get over to that one. I stumbled and things came crashing down. Me with it."

"That is a beauty," Fiona said. She examined Gilly's legs, running her soft hands along the bones and manipulating them. Putting just a bit of pressure here and there. "Bend. Bend. Good. Get up slowly."

Finn had cleared a pathway for them to get away from the carriages. He hadn't said much since Fiona yelled at him. Gilly did remember to thank Finn as he stalked away, heading toward the stallions.

"Finn, this is your fault!" Magnus bellowed.

He held his hands out. "How—is it my fault, Magnus? I didn't force the stupid filly in here." He kicked the floor.

"I told you to chop up the Beasts and use them for firewood. They are of no use to us and are dangerous. I've told you, in our history, horses have died because of humans and their Beasts. I intend to be rid of them all."

Fiona and Gilly hurried to the doorway. "No!" Fiona shouted. "These are valuable. They're antiques."

Ronan snorted. "You heard Magnus. Chop and burn the mess. And think how warm you'll be this winter." He sneered.

Fiona was trying to think of something to say. She bit her lip.

"We—we can't burn the wood inside."

Everyone looked at her, even Finn.

"Why?" Ronan looked angry. He didn't want to look like a fool in front of Magnus, challenged by a human girl.

Gilly recognized the look when a thought popped into Fiona's head. Her eyes widened and she had a slight smile. "It's—it's the paint and varnishes. They're toxic. The fumes would kill us."

Finn snapped to attention as if he'd just woken up. "Yikes. I never thought of that. She's right."

"Is she now, boy?" Magnus took over. His eyes narrowed and he laid his ears back. "Then you'll be chopping day and night, night and day." He whinnied a laugh. "Chop up the Beasts and burn the lot outside. A bonfire, is that what you call it? And keep chopping your precious trees for warmth inside this winter." He sniffed the air. "Smells like we're going to have a frigid one." He galloped away. Ronan and Lorcan followed.

Fists clenched and head down, Finn ran from the Carriage House.

Gilly looked at Fiona. "I'm sorry. I keep causing trouble for you."

She sighed. "You're young. You'll learn." She threw her arms around Gilly's neck and squeezed. "I still love you." She felt the warm blood. "Let's get you cleaned up and have you stay with Brora."

Fiona came back to the Carriage House after getting Gilly settled. It was hard to tell how late it was since the day was gray and a fine mist persisted after the earlier downpour. Exhausted, a chill ran through her. *I hope Magnus is wrong about winter being so cold.*

She heard the unmistakable sound of chopping inside. She entered the Carriage House and gasped. Finn was intense, swinging an axe, like a crazy man. "Finn, stop!" She ran over to him and the mangled wagon. At least he'd gotten started on a wagon that was beyond repair. *Whew.* "Hey, don't let Magnus push your buttons. Come on, let me help." She sat on the back of a buckboard, glad that it held her weight.

He took a deep breath and joined her on the buckboard, axe still in hand. The buckboard groaned with the new weight.

"Hey, throw the axe down. The added weight might do us in. We'd be looking foolish like Gilly."

Metal clanged to the ground, and he laughed.

She felt the tension lift. They sat side-by-side, shoulders slumped, feet dangling.

"Finn, I'm here for you. What do you need me to do?" She put her arm around his shoulder and waited a moment. "I think I understand your loyalty to the horses."

"Do you?"

"You're just trying to protect them?" She looked into his green eyes. "Sometimes we need to make the best of what we have."

"Fi, you've really grown up since the fi—fire." He looked away. "I hate myself."

He's still sensitive…he can't be completely brainwashed. "This fire that Magnus wants you to have, not a good idea. Huge bonfire—airplanes—discovery. The castle, the horses, us. Unless you want the horses to be discovered? But we would be rescued! And then we can prove your innocence."

"As usual, sis, good point. I'm not ready for all of that. I'll have to see if I can get Magnus to understand about the bonfire."

"And what harm are all of these carriages doing anyway?" She scanned the contents of the Carriage House in awe. *Wow! The ribbons we could win, Gilly and I.*

Mother Knows

Fiona leaned the shovel against a wall in the stables and studied her hands. No longer soft and youthful, they looked and felt like man's hands. There had to be a joke in there somewhere. She chuckled. Brora, several stalls along the aisle, cleared her nostrils and munched on hay. She knew that Brora was content to stay in the stables and not have to compete with the younger mares and stallions grazing in the fields. *Did she hear me laugh?* Fiona exhaled and watched it disappear. Morning frosts were a daily thing. "Winter is on the way." *It could snow any time in the mountains. Thanks to Finn I won't freeze: warm coat, boots, and gloves.* "A hat would be nice, next time you're in town."

"Did you say something, dear?" Brora called from a distance.

"Just talking to myself." She smiled. Fiona hefted a

pile of manure into the wheelbarrow. She stopped again, peered out of an archway and gawked at the intense red and orange leaves on a sugar maple. *It's got to be mid-October by now.* It dawned on her how quiet it was in the barn. "Brora, have you seen Gilly?"

"I heard Lorcan and her whispering earlier. Something about Finn and hunting."

"They'd better stay out of his way or he'll be pissed if tomorrow's dinner gets away." Her knees quivered. *Why do I let him get to me?*

The clatter of hooves getting louder prompted her to put the shovel aside. She ran to the back courtyard to see Gilly and Lorcan, vapor escaping from their nostrils, heading her way. "Slow down. Slow down." She held her hands in the air. "Whoa!"

The pair slid to a stop on the cobbles inches from her. They snorted and pranced around.

Hands on hips, Fiona asked, "What did you do now?"

"Us," they said in unison, looking at each other. Steam shrouded their faces.

Fiona scowled and tapped her foot. "Out with it."

Brora clattered toward them. Her head came past Fiona. She jumped sideways and watched her nip Lorcan.

"Hey, what's that for?" Lorcan whined.

Gilly laughed. Brora shot her a menacing look—ears back, teeth bared.

"Why do you always think we did something wrong?" Gilly pouted.

Fiona approached Gilly. "You two equal trouble." She continued tapping her foot. "Well? And I want the truth." *As Brora had said to her.*

Gilly pawed the ground. "We followed Finn. And Lorcan couldn't help it—"

Lorcan snorted and gave her a look.

"—And that's what happened. He didn't mean it. The snort, I mean. Dust gets up his nose all the time." Gilly hung her head. "A rabbit got away from Finn, and he chased us."

"True, Lorcan is sensitive to dust and now apparently leaf molds, given the time of year," Brora said.

Fiona put her hands to her face. "Finn will be impossible later. I'll have to stay out of his way. And that goes for you two." *Finn was never this moody before. I suppose it's all about survival out here. He's so serious and brainwashed. I bet a shrink would have a field day with him.*

"Gilly, what you need are training sessions, like we used to do back at the farm. You've had far too much freedom and no responsibilities since we've gotten here."

Gilly tossed her head and gave Fiona a head butt.

She looked at Brora. "Not my place to train Lorcan, I guess?"

Brora shook her head. "Lorcan will learn his place

in the herd from his father. I am only his mother. I gave him life and nurtured him. He runs with the stallions now. It's not my place to interfere. Nor yours! Remember what Magnus said. 'Humans are not to control us.' You and the boy are here at the pleasure of Magnus, to serve us." Brora lowered her head, embarrassed, and snuffled Fiona.

"Would he really kill me?" Fiona gulped, as a chill ran down her spine.

Brora looked at her with big brown eyes. "I'm afraid so."

"But Gilly…? She's mine, I can—"

"She belongs to the herd and will be Lorcan's mate when they are older."

Lorcan pranced around Gilly with his head and tail held high. Gilly kicked at him, and missed.

"I'm too old to foal," Brora continued. "I'm afraid Lorcan was my last…" She looked wistful. "The few mares are getting on in age. Gilly is our hope for the future. She brings a new bloodline into the herd. Destiny has brought her here, so that we can survive."

"Eldar told me I would change destiny." *Was this herd meant to die off? Lives would be lost. Mine? Finn's?*

"I think I understand," Fiona said. Tears welled up in her eyes. Emmeric was right. 'Don't get attached…' Either way, Gilly was never mine.

"Who is Eldar, dear?"

"A wise old owl, whose advice *maybe* I should have taken."

"Gilly replaces the one that esc—uh, left us many seasons ago. Also a Haflinger, come to think of it," Brora said thoughtfully. "A pretty little filly with a lot of spunk, like our Gilly. Hmm, what was her name? Donna, Donato…"

Fiona felt her face flush, and she stepped back, tripping over a cobble. She found herself sitting on the ground. Hands splayed out at her sides. "Danuba?"

"Yes, that was it. Danuba!" Brora declared. "How did *you* know that name? Do you know her? How?" Brora pawed the ground.

Fiona's heart jumped into her throat. "Sh—she's G—Gilly's dam, uh—I mean, mother. How? It can't be. But. She lives at Quimby Farm."

Fiona felt her head spin.

"Are you okay, dear?" Brora snuffled Fiona's hair.

"I—I don't know."

Gilly trumpeted a loud whinny and reared up in excitement. "My mother was here? She lived here?"

Brora chuckled, "Yes, for a while."

"I knew it. I told you that I loved this place, Fiona." Gilly pranced.

Fiona couldn't hold back the tears. Now she knew. She'd lost Gilly for good. She ran from the courtyard into the castle, and tripped up the steps to her bedroom, flopped onto her bed and bawled her eyes out.

Gig

Gilly whinnied and snorted in the main courtyard, the sound echoing. She hadn't seen Fiona for days. She was so upset that everything she ate tasted bitter. Gilly ran to the stables. "Tess. Tess."

Tess followed by Tilda and Pip rounded a corner, tongues lolling, out of breath and barked greetings.

"What is it?" Tess said.

"I'm worried about Fiona. I think she's still mad and is avoiding me—all because I want to stay here?"

Tess nodded and looked thoughtful, but said nothing.

Brora clattered into the courtyard and nosed Gilly. "What's the matter?"

"It's Fiona. She's dodging me. She won't even look at me," Gilly said.

Brora nickered in sympathy and smiled at Tess.

"You'll work it out," Tess said.

"I don't like this," Gilly said. "No petting. No brushing. No treats. No long girl talks. No sharing daydreams about winning ribbons and medals at shows..."

"That's all changed. Your decision has put an end to Fiona's dream and from the sound of it, your dream too. It will have to be another horse and another time—if she ever leaves," Tess said while eyeing Brora.

Brora nodded. Her big brown eyes were soft with compassion. "You two share a special bond. Don't let your decision destroy it."

"What can I do to fix things?"

"Go. Talk to her," Tess said. Her tail wagged.

Tilda gave a playful nip to Gilly's leg. Pip head bumped Gilly.

"Stop, Tilda, Pip. I'm not in the mood," Gilly said. She flicked her tail at them.

Tilda returned to her mother's side, tail tucked between her legs. Pip wandered back toward the sheep pen.

Gilly looked back at Tess. "But Fiona won't even come to me." Gilly hung her head low.

"I know exactly where she is right now, the Carriage House." Tess nipped at Gilly to encourage her to move. "Get going. Make the first move, now!"

I can't be mad at Tess for the nip of encouragement. Oh, well. I'll try...

A short time later Gilly snuck up to the arched doorway and peered into the Carriage House. Her body hugged the cold stone wall. She slowly peered around the corner, her eyes adjusting to the cavernous darkness inside. She spotted Fiona, slowly meandering along a row of carts, running a hand along each one. Petting it. Quietly whispering to the carts. Gilly couldn't make out what Fiona was saying, and perked her ears forward with all the concentration she could muster. She looked so sad. Her head was down, shoulders bent over. *I have to go to her...will she talk to me?* Gilly waited a few more minutes, sucked in a big breath, and walked into the open doorway where she knew she'd be spotted once Fiona looked up.

Fiona noticed her then quickly looked away. She put both hands in her pockets before turning her back. She walked away.

"Fiona...please! Stop," Gilly pleaded.

Fiona spun around. "Why? You've made your choice. You have a new friend." She kept walking.

Her voice held a vile bite of anger. Something Gilly had never heard before from her mistress. "Wait. Wait." Gilly picked her way gingerly among the carts. She didn't want to repeat her previous cart mishap.

She caught up to Fiona. She nudged her arm in the hopes that it would loosen her hand from her coat pocket. Fiona held fast. She nudged again and the hand flew out this time but Fiona put it by her side. A frown appeared on her face.

"I did this for you! To save you." Fiona shook with anger.

Gilly's mind raced. "Yes, you did…and *here we are,* just like you planned. Was—wasn't this supposed to be our always and forever home?"

Fiona threw her hands up in the air. "But it wasn't supposed to be like *this.* No Finn. No 'nasty horses.' And I feel like I'm losing you to Lorcan."

Silence.

Fiona's face reddened from yelling. She was silent now. It took a few long moments. Her expression changed from anger to a questioning gaze, then finally understanding.

"Oh, Gilly! How could I be so stupid? Please forgive me." She threw her arms around Gilly's neck. "It's not your fault. I led you here. Me! Stupid me. And it's only natural for you to be with other horses."

Gilly felt wet tears and runny nose on her neck. She nudged Fiona, nickered and licked her face. She eyed the carts and had a thought. *Wait till tomorrow.*

♥

"Lorcan, you're getting on my nerves," Gilly said.

"What's wrong, you two? It's going to be a lovely day. Go out and play when you're done eating," Brora said. The low early morning light forced its way through tree branches and archways, spilling into the aisle of the stables.

Gilly heard Fiona singing several stalls down along the aisle. Gilly flipped her tail back and forth, happy that they had made up. *If my idea works, she'll be thrilled. She'll be so happy that she'll forget all about Finn and the other horses.*

"Brora, if it's okay I'd rather spend some time with Tilda and the sheep. I've been ignoring them lately. They're my friends, too."

Brora bobbed her head. "I understand, little one. I'll send Lorcan out to Magnus. We girls could use a break." Brora whinnied.

Fiona stepped out from the kitchen door and down the steps, food scraps in hand for the chickens. High noon, she shivered as a blast of cold air whipped past. It was as warm as it was going to get today and she'd left her coat in the castle. "Here chick-chick-chick. Here chick-ees." Chickens flew and ran at her from all directions, from the stables, from under bushes and near naked tree branches. They clucked and crowed at her feet in anticipation of the treats she was about to scatter. A new group of sounds joined in to create a cacophony—bleats and barking and hoof beats. She stared at the barnyard scene in front of her. Recent memories of Rose, Emmeric, and Quimby Farm flooded her mind.

"Is there a party and someone forgot to send me an invitation?" She looked out past the chickens to where Gilly, Tilda, Pip, and the other sheep stood on the cobbles.

"Sort of," Gilly said.

Tilda barked excitedly, and the sheep scattered.

Fiona giggled. "It's okay, girls. Come on back."

"I had a thought," Gilly said. "Follow me."

"Wait, I need my coat." Fiona was back out the door in a flash, pulling down the new knit hat that Finn had brought her. She shoved her arms into the sleeves of the coat and ran down the steps. She squashed her pony tail under the hat and jumped onto the cobbles, almost twisting an ankle. The chickens scattered back to their hiding spots.

The sheep regrouped. They all followed Gilly through several arches, through the stables, and out into the main courtyard.

"You've got my curiosity. What's up?" Fiona asked.

"You'll see." Gilly trotted around the group, head held high. She headed to the Carriage House and stood in the doorway. "Tah dah!"

Fiona looked around searching for something new and different. "Yeah, and what are we here for? And why the audience?" She looked at Tilda, little Pip, and the sheep.

Yan replied, "We are to be… your cheerleading squad. Whatever that means." The sheep baaed in unison.

Fiona watched Gilly, carefully picking her way among the carts and wagons.

"Which one, Fiona? Which one?" Gilly said.

"What do you mean?"

"Which one can I train on? Which one to win the blue ribbon?"

Fiona gasped. "I—I want to. But I can't. Magnus's rules. We can't, Gilly."

"Sure we can. Magnus will never find out. The stallions are so far out on the property. I've spied on them. I know where they go. I ditched Lorcan today. And besides, who here is going to tell?"

Fiona thought. *I could do my training with Gilly in secret. Especially with Finn gone hunting or to town during most of the days. And still get my chores done. Hmmm…*

She grinned and pointed beyond where Gilly stood. "A gig. We'll start out with a gig."

Defiance

"What have you been so busy with lately?" Finn asked casually. He took a spoonful of soup. A scowl of mistrust lingered on his face.

"Me? Uh…straightening the stables and reorganizing things for winter." A piece of dry toast stuck in her throat when she swallowed. A swig of coffee helped it along.

"More than tidying up the place, from what Magnus said." His scowl of mistrust changed to a glare of anger. "You really managed to piss him off today. Now he'll take it out on me and make my life miserable. More insane chores, like following him around with a shovel and picking up hot stinky manure right after he's—"

"You've done that? Why?" But she knew the answer. Magnus had no love for humans and would do anything to demean Finn and her. Her thought shifted back to why Magnus was angry now. "What—what did I do?"

Finn raised his voice. "How 'bout the fact that you cut the manes on the mares today. Not just Gilly. The others too. Didn't you think the stallions would notice? Are you running a beauty salon for horses?"

"I—I didn't mean any harm. It was just a trim. The bridle paths and forelocks. So that I could brush them easier. I wasn't trying to get you into trouble. Sorry."

"Bridle path. Whatever that is." He gave her a sharp look. "I hope you're not planning anything stupid with bits and bridles or whatever you call that horse gear stuff. I notice you hanging out in the Carriage House. Magnus isn't kidding around. I've seen what he's capable of. He killed another stallion..." Finn's voice trailed off.

"Have you seen Ronan around lately?" he said suddenly.

Fiona gasped and sat back in her chair. "No!"

"Yes. Not a pretty picture to be kicked and stomped to death. Every bone in Ronan's body was broken."

"You watched?"

"I had no choice. I was there when the fight broke out. Something about trust and Lorcan and I don't know what else...I had to help drag Ronan's huge body into the woods along with some of the other stallions." Finn had a dry heave. His face turned white.

Fiona put her hands to her face in horror. "I'm so sorry, Finn. I didn't know he was *that* dangerous. I thought it was all macho acting." *I really need to be careful. This is no game.* "Shou-should I apologize to Magnus tomorrow?"

"No! Stay out of his way till his mood improves. Give it a few days. I'll have to do his bidding in the meantime."

"What can I do to make things right with *you*?" She felt her face redden and looked away.

"Stick with your chores and anything else he wants you to do. Don't get any creative ideas."

Fiona forced herself and said brightly, "We should have more talks. Er, not like this one, but more...like we used to. Before the f-fi..." *Don't say it!* "Seems like we only spend meal times together. Are you sure I can't come to town with you or come along hunting? How about playing cards at night? I found a deck in the library—"

"No. You need to stay here and tend to your chores. I can handle my own."

"That's not what I mean." She looked him in the eyes. "I know yo-you can do your work. It's just...I just...can't I give you a hand at least?" *Can't we be sister and brother again?*

His eyes were that of a stranger's. They held a faraway glower. They held no warmth, no joy, and no hint of shared childhood secrets.

"Finn, I'm sorry you had to watch Magnus kill Ronan. I can't even imagine how you handled helping to drag his body away..." *Let me go out on a limb here...* "I—I love you." She tried to catch his eyes. No luck.

He pushed his chair away from the table and got up. He turned to walk away, stopping for a second. "The soup was good. Put a log or two on the fire in your room tonight. It'll be cold. Frost in the morning..." His voice trailed off. He walked out of the kitchen into the library.

Fiona picked up the dishes from the table. Tears welled up in her eyes, making clean up a blurry task. The last dish put away, she ran from the kitchen and the conversation they'd just had. She passed through the chilly library and tripped up the dark winding steps to her room in the tower. *Damn I forgot the lamp, to see where I'm going.* Fiona closed her bedroom door and ran to the dresser, shakily lighting a couple of candles. Her sad face stared back from the mirror. Pulling a cloth from her pants pocket to wipe away tears, a flaxen bundle landed on the floor. She bent down to pick up the knotted mass. A tear fell off her nose.

She laid the flaxen mane—Gilly's mane—on the dresser and opened the top drawer to find the bundle of red hair—Finn's hair. She laid them side by side. The candlelight bounced back from the golden-yellow and red bundles. Fiona jimmied the lower drawer open, carefully pulling the Memory Box out. A yellow ribbon caught her eye. She unwound the beautiful ribbon and tied it around the hair bundles and divided them into three sections.

Before she knew it she held up a braid and turned it around in her hand. Candlelight reflected the red and golden-yellow in the mirror. She re-tied the ribbon to secure the braid into a band. *No matter what happens I have this as a keepsake.* She sniffled away the last tear.

Fiona groped under her bed and found what she was looking for—her backpack. She kissed the circlet of hair, unzipped the pack, and then gently stowed her treasure into a zipped compartment. She slid the pack easily back under the bed.

♥

How did he know it was going to be so cold this morning? Fiona could barely stand the wet washcloth on her face. "Ahh!" Her room felt freezing despite the extra logs at bedtime. The fire had died out. All that remained was cooling embers. She quickly wriggled into a pair of canvas pants and layered on shirts and slipped a sweater over her head. *Two pairs of socks ought to do it.*

A chilly draft swirled up the winding staircase to meet her. She shivered and slammed her bedroom door closed on the way out to keep what little heat remained intact in the room. She ran down the steps, through the library and into the kitchen. She spotted an empty bowl and cup on the table. A box of cereal and a quart container of milk remained on the counter. He had already come and gone. A stainless coffee pot sat just out of reach of the burning embers of the kitchen fire. She bent down and touched it—still warm. Liquid sloshed inside the pot. She edged it closer to the heat. She smiled at the thought of Finn making coffee for her.

Fiona knew she hadn't overslept. But this cold weather made the animals hungrier. Not taking the time to eat like a lady, she gulped down her cereal and slurped milk from the bowl. *Real Mom and Adoptive Mom Rose would not approve of such un-lady like behavior.* She carried a piping hot mug of coffee, spilling and sipping as she made her way across the cobbles to the stables. Months ago she could never imagine ever drinking the stuff. "Rats! Waitressing is not in your future, Fiona." Chickens clucked as if in agreement and scattered out of her way.

"Good morning, girls," she called out from the aisle in the stables. The sheep bleated greetings but the mares answered in subdued, quiet nickers. Finn's conversation from last night popped into her head. She stopped in her tracks, and shook the thoughts aside. Her mind made up, nothing would change it. Not even Ronan's death. She felt goose bumps. Gilly was still hers.

Tess and Tilda came barreling around the corner bumping into her. Coffee sloshed from the mug. "Hey, careful."

"Sorry," Tess said. "I hear from Brora that you're in trouble with Magnus."

"Finn told me last night. Magnus doesn't care for my grooming the mares. That is, the haircut part."

Brora ambled along the aisle. "I tried to warn you."

Fiona felt her face flush. "But you all look so much better, and it'll be easier to brush."

"All a matter of opinion, I suppose," Brora replied. "I'm hungry." She turned around heading back to her stall.

"Okay, okay, hold your horses."

The dogs sat at Fiona's feet, their ears cocked forward.

Fiona turned in time to see Gilly sneaking up on her.

"Is today the day? When?" Gilly asked.

"Shush. It's our secret. We can't let the other horses know, not even Brora. Gilly, meet me when you're done eating. You know where."

Tess gave Fiona a look of concern.

"I know what you're thinking. But this is something I have to do. There's no way Magnus will ever find out if we all stay quiet. What. Stop that. Gilly is still mine!"

Tess shook her head un-approvingly and walked away. Tilda stayed with Fiona, tail wagging.

"Okay. That's all done. Everyone's fed and watered," Fiona muttered as she hung a pail on a hook outside of a mare's stall. I should have everything ready by the time Gilly shows up." Fiona wiped her hands on her pants. *I've picked out the good leather and cleaned up the harness pieces... the gig's dusted off...all the mares had a trim... that should throw off any suspicion that I'm only working with Gilly. I wish Finn hadn't seen me in the Carriage House. Thank goodness he's too busy to chop up any more carts. Does he suspect?*

Fiona grabbed the empty coffee mug. "Hey, Tilda, would you mind running the mug to the kitchen door for me? I'll put it inside later."

"Sure. Do you want me to meet you in the Carriage House?" Tilda said.

"You may as well wait for Gilly to finish and then you could both come. Be on the lookout for Lorcan and Finn and the stallions. Make it look like you and Gilly are heading in another direction if they show up."

Tilda barked with anticipation. "Can I bring the sheep, too?"

"Not today. I don't need Gilly more nervous on her first day. It'll be stressful enough. Maybe next time." Fiona handed the mug to Tilda and pulled her sweater up to her neck, bracing herself against the morning chill. She hugged the side of the building and made her way through the main courtyard to the Carriage House and the stash of parts waiting to be assembled and hooked up to a novice filly for the first time.

Green Broke

Gilly heard clack-clack-clack coming from the courtyard before rounding a corner to see what the racket was about. Fiona was having a time of it, dragging the gig and harnesses behind her, over the cobbles. Clack-clack-clack. The two wheels on the gig had a mind of their own—catching in the ruts between stones. She turned around. Her tongue stuck out in concentration. She struggled to free the cart, changing direction in the process. She zigzagged along. She looked frazzled. A straight line would have been faster.

"Wonder where she's headed?" Tilda said. She looked up at Gilly.

A clump of harnesses fell on the ground. Tilda ran over and picked up a mouthful of leather.

"Thanks." Fiona gently laid the shafts on the ground and hefted the pieces back onto the gig. "Let's get out of here and onto less bumpy ground." Fiona jutted her chin toward the main arch. "Besides, this noise is bound to be heard, echoing off all the stone. We don't want that."

Gilly, trotted past her friends and the gig through the stone arch to the outside. She smelled the grasses and pawed the ground. "Ah, much softer out here." She nodded in approval. But just as quickly began pacing. Her stomach felt loopy with nerves. *I don't know if I can do this. I'm not ready. It's scary...* The gig looked bigger than life-size as it approached. Gilly's worries felt like a tightly wound spring ready to let loose.

Fiona wore a soft smile of understanding. Her words were soothing too. "Gilly, nothing to worry about. Come and smell the gig and harnesses." She patted the side of Gilly's neck. "Walk over here too." She led Gilly by her mane all the way around the cart.

Gilly exhaled a deep breath. The spring uncoiled a bit.

Tilda ran around the cart and between Gilly's legs, managing to escape her hooves.

Fiona grabbed a piece of leather. "I'm going to put this on your back."

Gilly's eyes widened.

"It's no different than the duffle bag and backpack that you've been carrying. You did that all summer long and throughout the journey. Piece of cake," Fiona said.

She slid the narrow band of a saddle onto Gilly's back and adjusted it back and forth to center it. "Tilda couldn't even sit on this. I don't know why they call it a saddle."

"That's it? I hardly feel anything." The spring uncoiled some more.

Fiona untangled the long straps and buckled them onto the saddle. She placed a strip of leather across Gilly's chest and did some more buckling and pulling. "Now for the head stall."

Gilly shrank back, away from Fiona.

"Gilly, it's just like—" Fiona slipped it over Gilly's head. "—a halter. Cool beans! You look like a real driving horse." She stood back to admire her work.

Gilly shrilled. "I can't see sideways! Help me!" She twisted her body and threw her head around.

Fiona grabbed her stomach and roared with laughter. "Oh, that's funny. I'm sorry, girl. I just can't…can't help it." She wiped a tear from her eye. "The expression on your face. I know it's not funny…"

"I still can't see sideways, even when I turn my head." The spring tightened!

"That's because you're wearing blinders. To keep you from being distracted when you're driving. You'll get used to them. All driving horses wear them." Fiona tapped her chin. "It's a fashion statement. You'll see like normal when I take the head stall off. I won't be hopping on the gig. I'll use voice commands from the ground. Any questions?"

"I don't like this. I feel trapped and foolish, like I have no control of myself." Gilly noted Fiona's hesitation in answering.

"That's the point," Fiona whispered.

I know that's why Magnus doesn't go for this. Gilly threw her head and pawed the ground. "We shouldn't do this. It's not okay, Fiona."

"You'll see. You'll love driving," Fiona pleaded, patting Gilly's neck before sliding all of the leather pieces off.

Gilly turned and slowly walked away. "I'm not sure now." Her voice faded.

♥

In the kitchen Fiona shed a pair of socks and the sweater. The afternoon air had warmed up. Perfect for training. The kitchen smelled like home. Rabbit stew simmered over a low fire. *I hope Gilly is as excited as me to keep going. She's doing really well and this is so much easier talking instead of me pushing her through the steps.*

"I finally get to do what I want to do," Fiona mumbled to herself.

"Which is what?" Finn said.

Fiona spun around from the fire. "Oh! You scared me. I didn't hear you coming."

"Late lunch. Dinner smells good," Finn said. "What do you finally get to do?"

"A-a new book that I spotted, that I can't wait to read." Fiona looked in the direction of the library.

Finn scowled. "That's nothing new. You're always reading." He quickly put together a peanut butter and jelly sandwich.

Think fast, think fast. "I found a stash of kerosene lanterns in the hayloft that I'm gonna clean up. They have wicks too. The added light will help me, us around the house."

"How did I miss finding them? Put the lamps out when you're not around. We don't have all the kerosene in the world."

"Absolutely." Fiona put on her perky voice.

"I'll be late tonight. Magnus has me shifting bedding from the summer stalls to the winter stalls which aren't as drafty."

"Great. See you later." Fiona gave a wave.

Finn turned to leave. The kitchen door banged shut.

Fiona stood next to the fountain in the courtyard and yelled, "Gilly! Gilly!" She tapped her foot on the stones and crossed her arms. "What's taking her so long?"

Gilly emerged through an archway into the court-yard, walking slow as a snail.

"What's up, girl? Aren't you excited? You're doing so well."

"What's the point, Fiona?" Gilly nuzzled her neck. "I feel foolish. We're here in the middle of no-where. There are no shows or blue ribbons or crowds to cheer us on."

Fiona pulled back. "Please, do this for me. For the challenge. To know that we can drive a fancy coach—*eventually.*"

"You know I don't have to do this. It's against Magnus' law. You can't make me," Gilly said.

Fiona felt the color drain from her face. Her stomach hurt. "This is all I've dreamed of. And you came to me, and suggested it." She paused. "Would you do this for me? I've talked about this ever since the morning I saw you standing on your wobbly new-born legs, with Danuba looking so proud. I want to prove that we can work as a team. That if you hadn't come here you would have had the potential to be a great driving horse." A tear fell down her cheek.

Gilly licked it away with her big sloppy tongue. Gilly hesitated. "For my friend. To prove a point. Yes. But, just this last time." She nickered.

Gilly didn't even freak out when the head stall went on with the blinders. "Here comes the almost best part.

Stand still. Don't jig around. Ple-e-e-ase." Fiona bent down and picked up the shafts. "Gilly, I'm gonna slide these along your side. I know you can't see what I'm doing. Trust me. I won't jab you. They're smooth. There you go. Good. I'll put them through the loop-ma-jigs. Done. A few more buckles and clips and we're good to go."

"That's it?" Gilly tried looking at her sides but couldn't. "They're stiff. I can't turn."

Fiona laughed. "I never thought about it. It's probably like wearing a corset. You couldn't bend at the waist. Let's try walking." She grabbed a hunk of mane. "How does it feel?"

"Not bad."

"We'll make a wide turn. Good. Try backing up. That's a bit trickier." Gilly pushed back. The gig's wheels creaked. "Not bad."

"I think I can get the hang of this," Gilly said.

"I'm gonna have you trot forward, then turn right and come back to me. On my command..." She watched Gilly's fluid movements. Her legs worked in unison, lifting and then extending down. Her hooves kicked up the dirt. "Beautiful. Higher on the legs. Higher. Now turn and back to me. Excellent!" Gilly met Fiona gently, head on. Their noses touched. "You're a natural. Go out further. Turn left. Try to remember to pick up your hooves like you're pulling them out of the mud."

"Like this?" Gilly held her head high.

"Great!" Fiona clapped.

Tilda barked and jumped in the air. "Go Gilly!"

"You've got it," Fiona yelled. "Yahoo! Yahoo! You did it. We did it." She yelled as she danced around. She yelled over the noise of the cart and hooves.

Gilly stopped short and shouted, cutting through the sound of Fiona's yelling and hooting. "Lorcan!"

"Lorcan? Where?" She spun toward the archway to see Lorcan. Too late, only now did she hear the echo of clattering hooves announcing his arrival.

Race to the Finish

Gilly skidded to a halt. The forward momentum of the gig pushed at her. She tried rearing up, but the stiff shafts and harness kept her on the ground. She whinnied. Shrill.

Lorcan's mass was framed in the arch. "I knew it. I just knew that you were up to something." Lorcan turned to leave.

"No. Wait. I can explain." Gilly walked toward Lorcan.

Lorcan spun around to Gilly. "Wait till Magnus finds out." He snorted and pawed the ground.

Fiona trembled where she stood, frozen to the ground, holding her hands over her mouth, to stifle a scream. Tilda crouched and snarled at Lorcan.

"There's nothing to explain. You've broken Magnus's laws. Forced by the girl? Tell me that you were forced." Lorcan hesitated; a wicked glint appeared in his eyes.

"Or did you have a weak moment and hope to *please* the girl? Which is it?" Lorcan's nostrils flared, his head held high in triumph. He stepped out of the shadow of the arch, toward Gilly.

Gilly looked at Fiona, then Lorcan. *What's the right answer? I'll either condemn Fiona or Lorcan will see me as weak. Either way, Fiona is doomed.*

"Actually." She thought for a minute. "It was my idea. I told Fiona to do it. I *demanded* that she do it!" Gilly held her head high to match Lorcan's posturing.

Fiona shot Gilly a look. *I hope you know what you're doing?*

Gilly nudged Fiona and whispered, "Be quiet." She turned her attention back to Lorcan, still blocking the archway. "You think you're the top colt here because Magnus is your father." Gilly sucked in a breath. *Here goes.* "I've got news for you. You're nothing!"

Lorcan stood, eyes wide, and reared up, almost hitting Tilda who had worked her way to circle him. "How dare you!"

Gilly nickered a laugh. "You know those stupid races we do out to the big oak tree and back?"

"Yeah?"

"I let you win!"

"Impossible. I have longer legs. I'm bigger."

"And you're a klutz. Your long legs get in the way. I

slow down when you stumble. I let you win!" It felt good
rubbing it in. "And this get-up, the gig and harnessing
looks ridiculous? You wouldn't have the nerve to try it."

*Gilly, you've either signed your own death warrant
or you're a genius.* Sweat dripped along her neck under
her mane. Her nostrils flared. She glanced at Fiona, who
looked like she was about to pass out. All color had
drained from her face. Gilly nudged Fiona and whispered, "Trust me. I *think* I know what I'm doing."

"What's the matter, Gilly? Your human doesn't look
so good." Lorcan gloated.

Gilly gave a gentle nip to Fiona's arm.

"Ouch. What's that—" Fiona said.

"You can't be serious," Gilly said, loud enough for
Lorcan to hear.

Fiona frowned, a puzzled look.

Gilly whispered. "Follow my lead. You would do that
for Lorcan?" She said a little louder.

"What are you two whispering about?" Lorcan asked.

"I don't know, Fiona. Magnus would have his hide.
And besides, he's such a klutz; I don't see how he could—"

"Enough! I want to know what you two are talking
about. What are you saying about me?"

An expression of understanding finally dawned in
Fiona's eyes. A smile spread across her face.

"You can do this, Fiona." They touched noses.

Fiona turned to Lorcan, "I think that you would make a grand driving horse." She looked at Gilly. "But, then, I'm not so sure. If he has such a hard time galloping, I don't think he'd have the coordination to trot pulling a wagon. It takes a magnificent horse to be able to drive like a *winner*."

Lorcan bucked and snorted, running in circles around Gilly and Fiona. Tilda ran for the bushes to avoid his raging hooves. "I can do it! I can do it!"

"I suppose," Fiona hesitated. "On one condition."

"Which is?" Lorcan stopped and stood, huffing.

"You can't tell anyone what we're doing. Deal?"

"Deal," Lorcan snorted.

"Now?" Fiona said.

"Now," Lorcan said.

Fiona undid Gilly from the gig and harnessing.

"Follow us to the Carriage House. If you decide not to, we'll understand. Right, Gilly?" Fiona winked.

That would be a shame. Beads of sweat reappeared along Gilly's neck.

Lorcan came to a halt outside of the Carriage House and shook his mane.

Fiona knew he was afraid. "Why don't you two go check that all's clear? That the stallions are far enough away." Gilly and Lorcan trotted off. "Tilda, check on Brora and the mares. I wonder where Tess is, too."

Fiona entered the Carriage House, picking her way through the aisles searching for a cart to fit Lorcan, and jockeyed a couple of carts forward. "I need him back here to size him to a cart." She looked outside. Afternoon shadows lengthened to bony fingers on the cobbles. "Not a lot of daylight left. They need to get back here." She shivered and spotted one of Finn's barn jackets hanging on a nail and threw it on. She heard the rapid clatter of young hooves getting closer. "About time."

"What about this one, Fiona?" Gilly nudged a Phaeton.

"Too big for him. I think a Meadowbrook is best. It's bigger than your gig and still has two wheels. Easier to turn than a four wheeler. A decent cart for a green horse."

"Am I still green?" Gilly asked.

"For a while yet…but then we're not doing this again."

Lorcan stood in the courtyard, shifting his weight from hoof to hoof.

"In here." Fiona stood straight, putting her hands on her hips.

He snorted before entering the Carriage House. His ears perked forward and eyes went wide.

"Just watch your footing. It's tricky maneuvering around." Fiona smiled at Gilly. She grunted, hefting a set of dusty harness pieces— made of heavier leathers meant for bigger horses—onto a Meadowbrook. They headed out to the courtyard. She really had a hard time pulling the heavier cart and harnesses across the cobbles. Clack-clack-clack. Louder than the gig. She scrunched her face. "Hey, you two, I need some help."

Gilly and Lorcan walked to the back of the cart. "What do you want us to do?" Gilly asked.

"Push. Push with your chests." Fiona pulled with all her might. Concentrating, she stuck her tongue out of the corner of her mouth. *A fifteen hundred pound horse would pull this along like a knife across butter.* All of a sudden, the cart moved more easily with the added horse power pushing. She didn't have to strain. *I hope all this noise doesn't bring Magnus and the others.* She steered it out of the courtyard and through the archway onto the soft grass.

"Lorcan and I better look to make sure Magnus isn't nearby," Gilly said.

"Quickly."

Clopping sounds followed Gilly and Lorcan across the cobbles, into the stables and out to the rear of the castle. The sound faded. Fiona sighed. It was quiet. She laid out the harnessing for Lorcan and the Meadowbrook.

Tilda barked excitedly. Fiona jumped. "I forgot you were there." She smiled.

The young dog danced circles around her. "What do you want me to do? Should I check on Brora and Tess?"

"Probably not a bad idea."

Tilda took off like a bullet.

Fiona needed two markers one at each end of the course so that the young horses could circle around them. What could she use? While crossing the courtyard she remembered seeing a jumble of cans, ropes and wood in a shed to the right of the Carriage House. There had to be something tall enough for them to run around in there. Her eyes adjusted to the darkness inside the shed. She rummaged through the dust-filled outbuilding until she found a heap of drop cloths covering something waist high. *That looks about the right height. Wonder what it is?* She lifted a corner of the canvas while holding her breath. Gasping for air, she rolled the cover back. Dust and old bird droppings floated up smack in her face. She coughed. "Sawhorses." Cough. "Great!" Gag. She hefted them from under the covers. She dragged them into the clear and hooked one under each arm and waddled back across the cobbles to the meadow grass.

She paced off a distance and set the sawhorses. The Meadowbrook cart and gig were lined up at what would be the start and finish line. The sound of hooves came clopping back through the courtyard. For a moment her heart skipped a beat. She took a deep breath, knowing it was only Gilly and Lorcan.

The horses blew air and snorted. "It's all clear. It's all clear. Magnus and the stallions are far away. We should be fine," Gilly said.

Tilda returned, panting up a storm. "We're in luck. Brora, Tess, and the mares are out in one of the pastures. I'm sure they're far enough away not to hear us."

"Okay, then, let's get started. First I have to hook you both up."

Lorcan jigged around nervously. "Is-is this going to hurt?"

Gilly whinnied a laugh. "Don't be silly, easy as oats!"

"Is that supposed to be funny or something?" Lorcan sneered.

"Don't bug him. It's going to be hard enough for me to work with you both at the same time. Gilly, stand in front of the gig. We'll harness you first, and this way Lorcan can see what we're doing." Fiona's nerves were on edge. She wiped her sweaty hands on her pants. *Where's Finn?* Could she trust the information from Gilly, Lorcan, and Tilda's scouting expeditions? Fingers slipped and fumbled with the buckles. She stopped tightening Gilly's girth strap. "Did you hear that?"

"Hear what?" Gilly swiveled her ears like radar.

Lorcan snorted and sneered, "Just some birds in the bushes over there."

Tilda ran to the commotion and flushed them into flight.

Chill afternoon air swept along her brow, making her shiver. *We don't have much time. It'll be dark soon. A few laps and that's about it.* Her teeth chattered as she finished hooking Gilly to the gig. "Next. Stand still Lorcan. Stop jiggling."

Lorcan pawed the ground. Some of the leather pieces fell.

Fiona wiped her hands on her pants, cupped them then blew warm air. "Do you want to do this or not? I could be inside reading a book by a warm fire." She crossed her arms and stared at the colt.

Gilly pranced proudly in place.

"Okay. Okay. Get on with it," Lorcan said, annoyed.

Fiona shortened the leathers which had been sized for a bigger horse then closed buckles and snaps. She double checked the old harness for brittleness. "It should hold. You're not pulling a cart with weight in it."

She took a quick look to the west. Dark gray clouds were moving in. The afternoon sun, now low in the sky, had a haze around it. Emmeric had taught her to be on the look-out for bad weather; cloud formations could spell the difference between life and death for young or weak animals out in a storm. Snow was on the way. She pulled her sweater collar up to her chin.

Her attention came back to the horses. "We'll walk the course together and then I'll let you try it on your own." She stood between the two horses at their shoulders and grabbed their manes. "Walk. Slowly. And try not to step on me, or squish me, please! Now. Walk." They made it to the distant sawhorse and circled wide to face the starting point. Lorcan's strides were longer than Gilly's which made it more difficult to keep them head-to-head. "Gilly, pick up the pace. Try to stay even with Lorcan. Better." Tilda gave Gilly a nip for inspiration.

Gilly looked contented, focused on the sawhorse in front of her. Lorcan was looking at everything but where they were headed. Fiona knew he was bored and nervous. "Listen; once I know that you two know what to do, I'll let you do it on your own."

Lorcan blew air and turned his head to snort, slobbering all over Fiona.

"Hey, not nice."

Lorcan gave her a wicked look. Gilly turned to Lorcan, pinned her ears back and bared her teeth to threaten a nip.

"Enough, you two. Let's call it a day."

"Aww, not yet. I'm having fun," Gilly said.

"He's not." They stood in front of the starting line sawhorse.

"This is stupid. I don't want you touching me. It's creepy. And you're making me go too slow," Lorcan said.

"Can I trust you to walk the course on your own? And I mean it. Walk. Nothing faster."

"Come on, Lorcan. Don't be a spoil sport," Gilly said. "I knew you couldn't do it."

"I can do it! Let's go Gilly. I'll show you," Lorcan said.

Fiona hesitated. Butterflies rose up with a vengeance from the pit of her stomach. She had a really bad feeling. It was too late. The horses walked past her and before she knew it, she was watching the backs of a Meadowbrook cart and gig heading toward the distant sawhorse.

"Remember what I said," she yelled out. Her eyes widened in disbelief. They had picked up speed. *Oh no!* The carts veered off course and headed toward the archway.

"No! Stop! Halt!" She ran with all her might to head them off. It was useless. Gilly and gig squeezed through the archway followed closely by Lorcan and Meadowbrook. The clop and clatter of hooves, and carts on the cobbles was deafening. The horseshoe shape of the courtyard acted like a megaphone. The sound magnified a-hundredfold and lifted skyward, propelled by the stiffening cold breeze. The clamor would reach the surrounding pastures and woodlands in no time. She reached the stone wall and stared with disbelief into the courtyard.

"Oh Gilly, Lorcan!"

In Pieces

As the horses rounded the fountain, the carts collided and the wheels interlocked. Fiona watched it unfold in slow motion, helpless to stop it. The crash was earthshattering, as loud as an explosion. Her ears rang from the scraping and twisting of metal and splintering of wood.

Pieces of carts and broken harnessing lay strewn around the base of the fountain in the center of the courtyard. Gilly and Lorcan were in a heap on the ground. Legs stuck out every which way. The screaming whinnies made her sick to her stomach. She cupped her ears. Her face felt hot and she bent over to wretch dry heaves. She held her aching stomach and ran as fast as she could to the wreck. *Stupid, stupid, stupid. They all tried to tell me.*

Finn, yelled from another archway, "What have you done?"

She couldn't turn to face him. The shock of seeing the horses in distress froze her next to the wreck. She stared and shook. "Help. Help me. Help them." Suddenly Finn grabbed her hand. She jumped.

"We have to get the horses undone fast before Magnus shows," Fiona said.

"Tell me what you need me to do," Finn said. "And then you have to leave."

"What?" She couldn't make sense of what he was saying. Her head spun. The horses were thrashing around and screaming.

"Fiona calm the horses. You're good at that."

"What? Oh." Fiona stepped gingerly among the debris and spoke softly to Gilly and Lorcan. "Finn and I will get you out. What hurts?"

Neither one answered. Their eyes were wide with fear and they snorted heavily as their chests heaved.

"We need to get the horses free," Fiona said to the dogs. "Over here. I need your help to lift."

Tess and Tilda pulled pieces from the rubble.

"There isn't much time. As soon as the horses are free, get in the house," Finn said.

Fiona gave him a look and opened her mouth.

"Don't argue with me. Magnus will demand that I

get you. They'll kill you." Finn pushed a shaft aside and unbuckled harnessing that hadn't snapped. He pointed to a strap. "Untie this."

Stampede.

Magnus and the stallions thundered into the court-yard. Magnus reared up, pawing the air as he surveyed the site before him. His snorts bellowed like a charging rhino. Gilly and Lorcan stood and shook out their manes. Their shrill whinnies continued.

Finn pushed Fiona. "Now! In the house. Tess, Tilda go with her."

Fiona ran toward Gilly, who backed away from her in fear.

"Fiona. Now!" Finn yelled.

"I love you Gilly." Fiona wiped tears from her face and ran for her life.

Gilly spun and galloped off with Lorcan through the stable arches.

Barking and snarling at the horses as they closed in, the dogs backed toward the house. Once inside with the dogs Fiona slammed the door closed and bent over exhausted.

A few minutes later she scrambled up the spiral steps, falling on her hands and knees on the way up. Her heart pounded in her ears. The dogs beat her to the landing. She slammed her bedroom door and looked out the window to below in the courtyard, praying that Magnus would not harm Finn.

"Fiona, you need a plan of escape," Tess said.

"But—I, but—I…need to save Finn."

"Think," Tess said.

Fiona took some deep breaths. Her lips trembled, fearing for Finn. The stallions were milling around, snorting and pawing the ground around the debris. Tails flailing, they were kicking out and yelling for her to come out.

"Fiona, think," Tess said.

Tilda jumped up and wagged her tail. She got on her belly on the floor.

Fiona heard something slide along under the bed. "What have you got, Tilda?" She met Tilda on the floor. "My backpack?! How can I escape from the horses with my backpack?" She sat Indian style.

Tilda pawed the top of the pack. "Open it."

Fiona reached in and rummaged around. Her hand grasped cold metal and she pulled it out, her slingshot. She smiled and threw her arms around Tilda, "You're brilliant." Pulling back on the leather thong, watching the band stretch she pictured a coyote in her sights. The coyote transformed into a horse. But these were huge horses. Not coyotes, the size of dogs.

She leaned her head back against the bed and closed

her eyes to think. "Tess, remember when the bats helped us in the orchard against the coyotes?"

"Of course."

"Batavia said that I could call on her any time. But it's late fall. They'd be hibernating. Do you think they'd come? How will they hear me from so far away?"

"I don't know. It may be worth finding out. Whatever you come up with it has to be fast. Can you trust Finn?"

Shivers ran up Fiona's spine. "I have to. His life's in danger because of me."

The sheep. I'm responsible for them too. A tremendous throb started above her eyebrows, the beginning of a painful headache. Moaning, she stood and made her way to the bedroom door. She ran up several more circular flights of stairs in the top of the west tower section. *Fiona you created this mess, and it's up to you to save and protect everyone!*

The sky had darkened. Chilled evening winds whipped her hair and her eyes watered. The wind whistled through the arched openings in the top of the tower. Years of snow and rain had blown into the space. Nests cluttered the rafters and piles of bird and bat droppings were all over. Wet moss underfoot made her slip. She went to an opening away from the main courtyard and inhaled deeply, careful not to lean into piles of droppings on the arches ledge. Cupping her hands to her mouth she yelled. "Batavia! Batavia! Batavia! Help us! Help us!" She waited. Batavia wouldn't come until it was too late… if she came at all. She thought with all her might.

What is Finn doing now? She went to the courtyard side and looked down. *The horses are still down there. They're not leaving. What is Finn going to do?* She ran back to the other side but her voice crackled and she couldn't feel her fingers. Her legs wobbled on the way back down the tower to her bedroom. *An escape plan for all of us…*

Fiona shivered. "Tess—I—I…"

"Take a minute to warm up," Tess said. She grabbed a blanket and dragged it to Fiona.

She sat in the wing back chair in her room, nodded and blew on her hands.

"I have a ver—very important job for Tilda."

Tilda wagged her tail. "What? What?"

"You need to quietly gather up the sheep without letting on that we're taking them away. Can you do this? I'm not leaving the sheep here."

Fiona turned to Tess. "Explain to Tilda where the path is that leads to town."

"What about Gilly and Finn?" Tess asked.

"I'm not sure. But I'm going to try to convince them to come. Finn is in great danger now. Gilly doesn't trust me. I need to get to the cellar." Fiona stuffed a hat, gloves and spare sweater in her pack and put her coat on. Hooking the backpack over one shoulder she hurried down the steps, through the library, to the kitchen. She lit a lamp and headed to the cellar. Holding the lamp up, she scanned the storage bins and shelves. There were sacks filled with potatoes and her bag of apples. She dragged two sacks of potatoes up the steps into the kitchen leaving one at the back door and taking the other to the front door. She ran back down to the cellar to retrieve the apples. Adrenaline kicked in. This was their only chance.

Would the bats even show up? The odds of surviving didn't look good. She stood in the kitchen clenching the bag of apples. The front door slammed shut and she jumped.

"Fiona!"

"I'm here. In the kitchen."

Magnus' Stand

Fiona clutched her bag of apples to her chest, shock waves racing through her body.

"Where are you?" Finn yelled.

"In the kitchen," she responded. It was the same feeling she remembered that hot summer day at the age of seven when she lost track of her parents and Finn at busy Faneuil Hall market in Boston. Waves of people had bumped and pushed her along. Dwarfed and alone, she yelled but her parents didn't come. She yelled for long, long minutes till her parents reappeared from the crowd. Her face tear soaked. Her parents reclaimed her with loving hugs and kisses. Finn rolled his eyes at the embarrassing scene made by his little sister.

"What are you doing?" Finn asked now.

Fiona closed her eyes and took a deep breath to calm herself. "That depends on you." *Just come out with it. I have to know.* "Will you help me, or are you bringing me to Magnus?"

Finn sighed. His eyes and face softened for the first time in a while since she'd arrived. *This was a real glimpse of her brother.* "I would never do that, turn you over to the horses. I already hurt you, in the worse way possible. I pushed you out the window. I killed Mom and Dad."

"You saved my life. The fire was a stupid accident. I forgive you." She put the bag down and reached for his hands. They were sweaty. "Come with me."

"We've been over this. There's no life for me outside." Tears welled up in his eyes. "You're better off without me. Go home where you belong. And learn to let go of horses. Loss is a part of life." Finn gave a half smile.

She grabbed him around his waist and hugged with all her might. She felt his warm tears on her head. "We're still family."

A few minutes passed, and Finn sucked in some breaths. "I'm afraid you're on your own. I can tell you what to expect. I can't do any more. I hope you understand."

"Do you know what he's planning? How many are there?"

"They've got both entrances to the Castle blocked. Three horses at each door. It's only the stallions. The mares won't be involved, that much I know. They'll be in the stables. And the last I saw of Gilly and Lorcan, they were petrified and hightailed it out into the fields. So they'll be out of the way."

She nodded.

"Oh, and they're prepared to wait it out if they have to. They realize you've got a limited supply of food and I'm forbidden to bring supplies in. I hope you've been thinking about a way to—"

Thump. Thump. Crack.

Tess ran to the front door and growled.

Fiona jumped. "What's that?"

"Sounds like they're kicking in the front door. Let me get out there and try to stall them." Finn grabbed her shoulders. "Punch me!"

"What?"

"In my face. Punch me. Hard."

She didn't know if it was rage or fear that she felt. Her ears rang. She clenched her fists and swung. Once. Twice. He stumbled back and landed on the floor. Blood oozed from his nose and lip. Unsteady, he dragged himself up off the floor. "Bye, Fiona. I do love you." He ran from the kitchen, through the library, dripping a trail of blood.

The front door slammed shut. She peeked out the kitchen window. Tess joined her, putting her paws on the window sill to look out, too. Clouds muted the moonlight which shone off the backs of three horses—as Finn had said would be there.

She slid down the wall and sat next to the sack of potatoes.

"Tilda should have the sheep in place by now. Hopefully she can keep them calm," Tess said. She licked Fiona's face. "Are you ready?"

Fiona felt numb. Already she missed Finn. A part of her expected to see him again, that he'd change his mind.

"If we get separated," Tess said, "head to the tall oak tree out back. The one that Gilly and Lorcan race around. A path begins a bit further down along the hedgerow. Follow this. It crosses roads. It'll take you to Bennington. I'll catch up."

Newly energized, she picked herself up off the kitchen floor and retrieved the bag of apples. "These belong at the front door—for our guest of honor." She slid over to a window in the foyer and peeked out to assess the situation. Magnus and two others, as Finn had said. Her brother was not in sight. *Probably in the stables tending to his wounds.*

"Tess, we'll start at the kitchen door and see how it goes." She opened the door just enough to extend half of her body. She grabbed a potato and slapped it in the slingshot.

Thwack.

A stallion reared up in shock and screamed out in pain, running in circles. The others looked at him.

Thwack.

Another horse reared up and screamed. The third ran into the stables. The two followed.

"That was too easy," Fiona said. Her mood lightened. Tess waged her tail.

Fiona opened the door again. Before she could make a run for it she heard Magnus bellow as he headed to the stables. His hooves clattered on the cobbles. "Get back here. Take up your positions."

"If you see her, kill her!" He bit each one of them hard before returning to the front courtyard. Fiona almost felt sorry for them.

"Should I try the horses in front?"

"May as well see what you're up against there," Tess said.

Remember what Emmeric taught you. Aim for the sweet spot. She took a deep breath, pocketed some potatoes and seated one in the slingshot. She opened the door slowly and peeked out, spotting two horses—not Magnus. Where was he hiding? She reached out with the slingshot and drew back with all her strength.

Thwack.

The potato hit one of the horses in the throat. He crashed to the ground.

A searing pain scorched her forearm. Screaming, she couldn't tear free. In a flash Tess charged and bit Magnus' leg. He had hid behind the door. Magnus stomped at Tess, but missed. He let go of Fiona's arm, and she pulled herself behind the door with Tess and slammed it shut. The slingshot clattered to the floor. Blood poured down to her fingers.

She slid to the floor. *Don't pass out.*

She woke to find Finn kneeling over her. Her arm was throbbing. She could see that her arm had been wrapped. Her coat was gone, sweater sleeve pushed up.

"Good thing you were wearing a coat and sweater. His teeth went clear through, and you've got a deep gash. You would have lost your arm otherwise," he said. "You need to go to a hospital when you get to Bennington."

"If…Bennington. How'd you…get in?"

"The stallions by the kitchen heard the commotion in the main courtyard and left their post. Magnus will probably have their hides. By the way, one horse is down in the courtyard."

"I…potato."

"Here take this for the pain."

She sat up and swallowed a pill and drank some water. "Slingshot."

"Right here." He handed it to her. "That's some weapon."

Thump. Crack.

"They're at the kitchen door."

"Help…up."

"Are you sure?" he asked.

She nodded even though she felt woozy and nauseated. "Coat…pack. Have to… finish this. Do they know… you're…here?"

"I don't think so. Why?"

"You're going to… be me." She winced with pain. "Slingshot time. Aim for windpipe. Ouch." Fiona winced slipping her arm into the coat sleeve. "Potatoes for stallions. Apples for Magnus. How many out front?"

Finn slid to the window and peeked out. "Two standing and one down. Magnus must be at the kitchen door now."

She showed Finn how to place the potato, pull, aim and release. Finn opened the door and pulled back on the seated potato.

Thump. Crack. Crack.

Hooves pummeled the kitchen door.

His shot missed and hit the cobbles behind the horses.

Splat.

Fiona watched the horses jump at the sound. "Give me…I'll do it."

She fumbled to hold the slingshot in her good hand.

The fingers in her bad arm felt numb while placing a potato in the pocket of the slingshot. Finn cracked the door open for her. She attempted to pull the slingshot, and pain like the scorching heat of a branding iron ran from her forearm to her fingers.

I can't do it.

She edged herself behind the door and dropped the potato and slingshot. He closed the door and scooped them up. She leaned against the door, holding tears back.

"Let me," Finn said.

"I can do it. Hold with bad arm, pull with good."

I have to.

Tess cocked her head, ran out of the foyer toward the tower section, and bolted up the circular steps without warning.

"Tess?" Fiona gave Finn a questioning look. In the quiet seconds that passed between them, the only noise came from the shrill whinnies and bold snorts in the courtyard. She gripped her slingshot. Finn's eyes widened. She saw how vulnerable he really was. He was a scared boy.

It was too quiet outside. *Was Magnus getting ready to attack and enter the castle?*

Tess flew down the steps two at a time. "It's them!" She panted loudly.

"Who?"

"The bats. They've come," Tess said. She wagged her tail as the three scrambled up the winding steps to the top of the west tower.

Fiona stepped out onto the tower roof top, the wind whipped her hair. She shielded her eyes with her good hand. Behind her, Finn's hair, too, was a red frenzy. Tess shook her coat out to trap warm air, looking like a fur ball.

"Batavia, is that you?" Fiona yelled at a massive black cloud swirling in the dark gray sky. The blob shape-shifted and broke apart. Fiona gasped. Hope rose up in her chest. "Batavia?"

A single black form came at her. Finn threw himself in front of her and waved his arms. "Get away from us." He pulled a potato out of his pocket and drew his arm back, poised to throw it.

Fiona grabbed his arm. "Stop. They're friends of mine."

"Huh?" Finn said.

"I know them. See." She turned to the bat hovering overhead. "Batavia?"

"Batavia sends her regards," the bat answered. "I'm Vega. You've passed from her territory to mine. She's asked that I assist you. Coyotes again?"

"No. Worse. Stallions are holding us hostage. I want to go home."

"Batavia said that you had left home with Gilly. Now you want to go home?" Vega asked.

Fiona sighed. "I made a huge mistake. I thought I was keeping Gilly safe and could keep her for myself. "I was being selfish." Her heart raced. "Can you help us?"

"There isn't much time. We've come out of hibernation and it's about to snow, in the next hour or so. We must hurry!" Vega answered.

A chill ran through Fiona and met the dull throb in her arm. "We'll help, too." She held up her slingshot. Finn hoisted a potato, and Tess bared her teeth.

Her voice lifted. "Vega, can you scatter the stallions? I'll take care of their leader, Magnus. We'll meet you on the ground."

"We'll do our best, but time is limited," Vega said.

Fiona ran to the kitchen door, Finn close behind. He cracked it open to let in the sounds of two stallions snorting an eerie battle cry. Pain flared up in Fiona's arm, dropping her to her knees. Tess bolted out the door, barking and snarling. "I can handle Magnus."

"Tess! No! I can't lose you."

Finn slammed the door. "She knows what she's doing." He knelt next to her. "Let's see what's happening in the courtyard."

Fiona forced herself off the floor and tore through the library to the foyer.

I'm not going to let Magnus win! If it's a fight he wants—

"Surrender, girl!" Magnus bellowed. "Surrender, and I'll let your dog live!"

She heard yelps of pain. "No! He has Tess."

"We'll get her back," Finn said.

"No, Finn. Get out of here. He doesn't know you've been helping me. Save yourself. Go!" She pushed him away and watched as he climbed the steps, a confused look on his face. "Remember Quimby and Fairfield. That's where I'll be." He disappeared around the bend of the steps. She pulled the front door open and stepped out into the night.

"Bats! What's going on here?" Magnus reared up. So did the other stallions. Tess ran up the steps to Fiona.

Amazed, Fiona watched the swirling black cloud shape-shift, break apart, change formations, and dive at the horses, who whinnied in fear and confusion. Tails swatted like mad. The cloud of bats was so thick the horses crashed into each other.

Some bats were hit by flailing tails and smashed into the stone wall of the castle. They lay dead on the cold ground.

"Stay in formation!" Magnus yelled. He stood firm, an example to his herd. Then he reared up, came down hard on the cobbles and charged at Fiona. His nostrils flared, eyes wide with rage.

Fiona bit back a flame of pain. He was almost upon her. She took two steps back and fired an apple at Magnus.

Thwack, splat.

An apple smacked into his shoulder, then hit the ground. Magnus stopped short.

His nostrils flared and twitched. She knew the sweet aroma would reach his nostrils. There, it had. He lowered his head mere inches, and then brought it up sharply, wary of the unexpected sweet smell.

Thwack, splat.

An apple hit his lower leg, then the ground, as she intended. These were not meant as kill shots.

His head lowered to the ground. His lips brushed the juicy sweet crushed fruit. He quickly pulled the apples into his mouth and chewed. No horse could resist the temptation of apples.

He was completely distracted from the bats and the stallions that the bats were driving off one-by-one.

Fiona smiled to herself despite the throb in her arm. It wouldn't be long now.

Thwack, splat.

Again and again. Too many to count.

She'd lost track. But knew he had eaten a lot.

The bats had disappeared and silence filled the courtyard. Fiona and Tess watched Magnus. He was getting lethargic, looked at his belly and attempting to kick it with a hind hoof. He wanted to lie down on the cold cobbles. Fiona felt in her pocket. Only two apples remained. She might need these for herself, for the journey. She walked down the steps and cautiously approached Magnus.

Magnus moaned. His legs buckled. He flopped on the ground, rolling from side-to-side. "What have you done to me, girl?"

"You tried to kill Tess and me. I never meant to hurt anyone here, and I'm not your slave! All you had to do was ask us to leave." She bent down and petted Magnus's head.

"How dare you touch me!" he groaned.

"That's your problem. You don't understand family and love. You want to control everyone. I'm going home."

She didn't have a chance to thank Vega and the bats who were by now, on the way back to their cave before the snowfall. If Gilly hadn't had the colic episode in the orchard the night of the coyote raid, she wouldn't have thought to use the apples as weapons. And Magnus the mighty ate many more apples than Gilly.

Still, she felt guilty that Magnus would probably die

from colic; a slow, painful death, even though HE had meant to kill her.

Journey

Fiona repositioned the pack on her back. "Ouch." The throbbing pain in her arm reminded her of how close she had come to losing it, and she still might without medical help in Bennington. They weren't clear of the courtyard.

"It's too quiet, Tess. Where are the horses?" She looked around and checked the sky for bats. Nothing.

"Maybe Vega and the bats are keeping them on the run to give us a head start."

"Let's hope." Fiona walked quickly toward the stables.

"Where are you going?"

"To say good bye to Brora."

Tess grabbed Fiona. "It's too dangerous. We need to go!"

Despite her pain Fiona walked faster, passing through the stable arches, determined, and thinking only of the hedgerow and big oak tree—escape. Sweat beads formed on her brow. She wiped her face before the cold air had a chance to chill her.

She heard voices up ahead. They were mere whispers. "Tess, check it out." She crouched down, waiting for her friend to report back.

"It's okay. It's Tilda and the sheep. We're ready now."

They reached the big oak tree, a darker shade of gray against the gray night sky. Everything appeared in shades of gray or black. "How will I see?"

"Your eyes will become accustomed," Tess said. "Hold on to the ruff of my neck. Pick your feet up so you don't trip. We'll be on a narrow path."

Fiona's nerves felt jangled. Her good hand shook when she grabbed ahold of Tess. She couldn't stop sweating from the fear and hurrying along and now she was blind as a bat. She would have to put her trust and faith in the dogs to get them to Bennington.

Finally, her night vision started setting in. She was able to pick out trees and branches, ducking and pushing them out of her way.

The air changed; a concentrated breeze brushed past her right shoulder. She was used to this by now. A dark swirl circled overhead. "Bats."

Vega fluttered by her head. "Miss Fiona, time for us to leave. The horses are gone far enough away for you to escape. The snow is approaching too quickly. Take care on your journey."

"How can I ever thank you, and Batavia, and all the bats?"

"You're a clever girl. I know you'll think of something." The dark cloud twirled, disappearing into the night.

Fiona and Tess walked side by side while the sheep walked single file. Tilda was last, nipping at Pip who wanted to lie down. They hadn't gone far when Fiona smelled a horrible smell. It got stronger. She took her throbbing hand, covered her nose, and winced in pain.

"Tess, what is that?"

"I'll go see." Tess came back awhile later, shaking her head and coughing. "What's left of Ronan."

Fiona looked in the direction of the stench. A branch hit her bad arm. Her neck hairs stood on end. "Let's get out of here."

The terrain sloped up through the mountains, and Fiona stumbled over rocks as fine snow began to fall. Fiona stuck her tongue out to taste the clean Vermont snow. She stopped and pulled her hat out of the backpack. "How much longer, Tess?"

"With the snow, probably five hours or so. The weather's getting bad."

Fiona held tight to Tess.

Tilda pushed and nipped the sheep to keep them from lying down in the storm.

"Keep them moving, Tilda. We can't lose any time in the mountains," Tess said.

"I'm doing my best," Tilda said.

Fiona reached out in front of her. The snowflakes were bigger now, faster. Snow quickly covered her coat sleeves. She slowed her walk.

Tess shook her head. "You're in no shape to stay here without supplies or medical attention. There's no telling how much snow's going to fall. But if I had to guess, too much for you to survive in."

Fiona grabbed onto Tess's ruff. She pulled her gloved hand away to see fresh blood. A result of Magnus biting her companion. "Never mind me. Tess, we need to get you to a hospital too!"

"Don't worry about me."

"Tilda, move those sheep along, quickly," Fiona said.

Fiona knew that Tess would die first before giving up her responsibilities. Fiona forced herself on, despite the chill that had reached deep inside her. She was charged with the care of her friends. And wouldn't let them down *now*. Her body shook. She stamped her feet while walking to keep the deep chill from settling in. The dry snow crunched under her boots. At least she wasn't slipping anymore, going up and down the hills. Tess promised that they had gone through the last large mountain pass. Flatter land and civilization were not far off.

Fiona's mind wandered to a hot summer's day. She was on a smooth sandy beach that lay between Lynn and Nahant, Long Beach. She wore a turquoise two piece bathing suit and held a reel of string. Her father was further along the beach holding onto a rainbow kite waiting for the right moment to send it soaring skyward. Fiona squealed with delight as her father teased her, "Now, Fi?" He had the biggest smile on his face. It was always windy at the beach.

Tess stopped abruptly. Fiona almost fell over her. "Tess?"

"I can't go."

"What's the problem?" Fiona spotted headlights coming towards them from both directions, traveling slowly in the storm. They found a major highway, now covered in snow.

"I almost died here, the time I followed Finn to town. I can't cross."

"Maybe they'll stop for us?" Fiona stepped onto the road and waved at the approaching headlights. They kept going. "No! It's not fair! They mustn't be able to see me." Anger replaced the chill. "We can all do this!" She looked at her friends. "When there's a break, follow my lead and make a run for it. Tilda keep everyone moving!"

She spotted houselights. People were waking. Fiona figured it was about 5:00am. No sign of a light tinged horizon yet. The sky remained snowy gray.

"Through the church yard and cemetery," Tess indicated.

They walked east along Route Nine. Fiona spotted a sign: "Welcome to Bennington."

"We made it?" Fiona asked.

No reply.

She'd never heard her friends *this* quiet.

A pickup truck drove past and blasted its horn. Fiona jumped.

The sheep bleated and ran out into the road. Barking, Tess and Tilda gathered them back onto the sidewalk. The snow fall slowed. Plows had gone through the main road but the sidewalk looked like it had six inches of crisp snow covering it. Fiona's feet were numb. She kept her eyes forward and reminded herself of the hot breeze at the beach. The chill was seeping into the warm spot in her mind, threatening to take that away.

Fiona, in a daze, almost ran into a man carrying a steaming cup of coffee and a newspaper. He scolded her. "You can't come into town with your livestock! There's an ordinance against that, missy."

"Police...department?" She stood shaking.

"Four blocks up, on your right. Kids these days," he shook his head and kept walking.

The sky seemed a brighter gray. Car horns blared. The sheep, bleating, had wandered into the street again. The dogs barked. Fiona barely had the strength to utter commands to retrieve the sheep. She trudged along in the snow, bumping into someone. "Hey watch it, kid." She turned the corner onto the fourth block, South Street, Route Seven according to the white sign. Across the street she spotted an imposing stone building with columns. A ramp lead up along the steps. *More gray stone.* Her mind felt dazed—frozen. *Move one foot, then the other...almost there.* "Ramp."

Tess crossed the street and stood by the ramp, barking nonstop.

Barking? No talking? Fiona tried to comprehend this.

Fiona struggled up the incline. Her mind ready to shut down, she had just enough strength to open the door. Tess wedged her body at the door, allowing Tilda and the sheep to enter. The dogs and sheep shook the snow off. Fiona stumbled up to the reception window and whispered, "Fiona Quimby."

The officer leaned toward her, "What did you say?"

"Fiona... Quimby." She slid to the floor, then heard a commotion but couldn't respond.

Murmured voices spoke. She heard her name. Hands

peeled off her backpack, coat, gloves, and boots. A male voice yelled, "Dispatch Bennington Rescue Squad paramedics to HQ forthwith. Female, teen, frostbite, extreme hypothermia and blood loss due to bite. Jimmy! Get me blankets."

Hands tucked blankets around her.

A beach towel?

"Meredith, run the name Fiona Quimby in the system," the male voice said.

"Comes back as a missing teen, out of Massachusetts, since August."

"Call the Massachusetts State Police. They'll contact her parents. Fiona will be a guest of Southern Vermont Medical Center for a while." He smoothed the hair from her face. "Hang on, honey, help's on the way. And call Animal Control."

Fiona tried to speak but couldn't. Tess and Tilda barked and lay on top of her legs.

"It's okay, girls. We'll take good care of your Fiona."

The man's voice was kind.

"You must have had some time of it over the last several months," he said.

Fiona heard more voices. Something pricked her, and she felt prodded, and jostled, then lifted into the air.

On her way to heaven?

Sound and feeling stopped.

Prodigal Daughter

"Fiona, can you hear me?"

She felt the voice deep inside her, as familiar as her own.

"It's me, Finn, checking on you. Hope you wake up soon. I've seen your new parents. They seem nice. You're lucky to have them. Magnus is dead. I think things will be better now and I'll be safe at the Castle. Gilly is fine." She felt his warm lips on her cheek. "Got to go. Bye for now."

Fiona swam up from the darkness. Warmth flowed through her hands. *It felt good.* She was lying on her back, in a soft bed. Covers pressed down on her legs and chest. Beeping sounds and whispers filled her ears. *The whispers were soothing.* Light pushed through her closed eyelids. *I want to stay in the darkness.* She wasn't ready to face the world.

"Fiona." A soft hand swept her forehead. "Fiona, it's me, Rose."

A firm hand squeezed hers. "And Emmeric."

She opened her eyes to the worried faces of her adoptive parents.

"How long have I been...where am I?"

"You're in a hospital in Bennington, Vermont. You've got some injuries, but you'll be fine."

Fiona spied an apple on the nightstand. She smiled to herself. *It wasn't a dream. Finn was here.* She wiped away tears.

"When can I go home? Do I have a home?" Fiona looked up at Rose and Emmeric. "You're going to send me to an orphanage. I don't blame you. I've been a terrible daughter. Why—why did you come?" Tears flowed down her cheeks. "You must hate me."

"Why would you think that?" Rose asked. "We don't hate you. We love you."

"We do," Emmeric said.

"Even after what I did? Taking Gilly and the dogs?"

"Always." Rose kissed Fiona's hand.

"Yes, we forgive you." Emmeric cleared his throat. "But I want to know—what happened to Gilly?"

"She ran off with a wild herd of Shires and drafts."

Emmeric sat back in his chair next to her bed. "So, they do exist. I always thought that was a rumor, a wild herd up north, breaking into horse pastures, stealing mares. I blamed them for Danuba's disappearance years ago—but she returned."

Rose rubbed Fiona's arm.

"I'm sorry. I shouldn't have taken Gilly. I was selfish. I wanted to keep her."

"No, you shouldn't have. But that doesn't change that we are your parents and you are our daughter." Emmeric leaned over and kissed her on the forehead.

Tears welled up in her eyes.

"And we'd love it if you called us Mom and Dad," Emmeric said.

Fiona looked away for a moment. "I remember everything."

Rose and Emmeric looked at each other. "What do you mean?" Rose said.

"I remember everything. Who I am. My family. My childhood. The fire. And I have a brother. I got my memory back."

"Then you know your brother set the fire," Emmeric said.

"Why didn't you tell me anything before?" Anger rose up inside her.

"The social worker in Boston wanted you to regain your memories on your own. She knew you would, but not when," Rose said.

Emmeric shook his head. "Your brother killed your parents and tried to kill you. He's wanted for murder."

"He didn't set the fire. It was an accident. Finn pushed me out the window to save me. He wanted to save our parents, too, but couldn't."

"That's not how the investigators see it," Emmeric said.

"Emmeric, no, you're wrong. They're wrong. One day I'll prove it."

Winter gave way to mud season. Fiona kept most of the details of her travels from Rose and Emmeric. They didn't need to know. She had kept Gilly from being sold but had lost her in the end. Gilly had decided her own future was with Lorcan and the herd. Finn now had a second chance to remain hidden from the world and remain safe at the Castle. She figured Lorcan would be in charge of the herd, he would rule with a mellow tone, influenced no doubt, by Brora and Gilly, due to his young age.

Fiona and Emmeric sat at the kitchen table, the dogs at their feet. Rose placed platters of scrambled eggs, bacon and toast on the table, a hearty breakfast on a cold, dark morning.

"We've got a good month yet before Danuba and Lileana foal," Emmeric said.

"Will the newborns be cousins?" Fiona asked.

Emmeric chuckled. "Half brothers or sisters, anyway. They share the same sire/father."

Fiona danced in her seat. "Can I name them? I won't get attached. I've learned my lesson. Promise." She crossed her heart.

Emmeric nodded, his mouth full of eggs.

"Emmer—Dad, can we do a father-daughter project before we get bogged down with the spring birthings?"

"It can't be too complex. We don't have a lot of free time coming up."

Rose gave Emmeric a look that he should listen.

"I want to build bat houses."

"Why bat houses?"

I want to remember the bats who lost their lives in battle with the horses.

"I've been reading up on them. They're interesting." She pulled a piece of paper out of her shirt pocket and handed it across the table. "I got this plan off of the Internet."

"They'll help keep the insects down," Rose said.

Emmeric glanced at the paper then laid it aside. "Okay." He eased back in his chair, sipping on his coffee.

"Now get upstairs and get bundled up. It's a nasty one today. We have a lot to do."

Fiona and the dogs raced up the stairs. At the top, Fiona tripped over Tilda and landed on her hands and knees. By the time she'd scrambled to her feet again, Tess had nudged her closet door open and pulled the Memory Box into the room. "What are you doing, girl?"

Tess barked and nudged the box with her nose.

"Tess, I miss our talks now that you're back to barking. You are like a best older girlfriend or sister. Thanks for helping me and saving me." She threw her arms around Tess' neck and sat on the floor Indian style to open the box. She took out the hospital I.D. band from Mass General—"Fiona Higgins"—and put it on her left wrist. She picked out the hospital band from Southern Vermont Medical Center— "Fiona Quimby"— placing it with the other band. Armed with the knowledge of her past she looked forward to her future. Then she pulled out the circlet of braided flaxen and fire red hairs, belonging to Gilly and Finn, held together with a yellow ribbon. She fingered the bracelet and held it up to the light. She smelled it before placing it on her right wrist, and then closed her eyes. "I miss them too, girls. Maybe someday we'll get a chance at being a whole family again." She returned everything to the box for safekeeping before going downstairs.

♥

April turned out to be a warm month. Fiona couldn't remember the last time it had snowed. Maybe early March. And without much rain, mud-season passed sooner than normal, and her tall Muck Boots sat unused by the back door. *Thank goodness the days are getting longer.* "Come on, girls. Tess! Tilda! Barn chores!"

Emmeric yelled from the lambing shed where Yan and Methra were about to give birth. "Don't forget to look in on Danuba and Lileana. Feel the rumps above the tails to see if they've softened. The teats should be waxy. Any day now."

"Okay, Dad!"

Fiona had a feeling that someone was in the barn when she entered. She spotted Pip by the horse stalls. But it was something else. Goosebumps ran up and down her arms. She walked cautiously toward the stalls. The horses nickered a greeting. Pip bumped her leg with his head. "Pip, you're on the way to being a handsome ram." She stopped first at Danuba's stall. Danuba approached and nuzzled Fiona's neck.

"Danuba, Gilly is safe at the Castle. She will have a mate. His name is Lorcan. Brora sends her regards."

Danuba nickered and nodded her head.

The dogs barked and ran past the stalls to the open

gable end door. Pip baa'd and caught up with the dogs. Tess and Tilda wagged their tails. Pip head bumped Tilda. Tilda yelped.

"What is it? Raccoons?" She was about to reach for the slingshot which was always in her pocket since she'd come home.

Something pink caught the corner of her eye by Lileana's stall. She turned and grabbed the stall door. She gasped, thinking she was having a vision but her touch confirmed it was real. Hanging on a hook was Gilly's bright pink foal's halter.

"Girls! He was here. Finn was here!" She grabbed the halter off the hook and ran to where the dogs stood at the gable end door. "Do you see him?" She held up the halter. "Finn was just here! He found us. I told him Quimby and Fairfield and he remembered."

"Finn come back! Finn!" She held the pink halter to her chest.

I know you're innocent Finn. I'm going to prove it!

♡

Acknowledgments

My interest in horses came by way of books. *Black Beauty* and *My Friend Flicka* among others. I was hooked. I had to graduate to the real thing! I was maybe eight-years-old when I was introduced to Francis "Fannie" Gardiner at the "Peach Farm" in East Hampton, LI, NY. Her ranch. A formidable woman. Tanned skin, western hat, wearing chaps—a real horsewoman! She lived and breathed horses. She taught me horse care from the ground up. Taught me to ride. But most of all, she taught me to respect horses—and so began my *love affair* with horses, thanks to Fannie. Throughout the years I rode or visited horses whenever, wherever possible. Always feeling that magical pull.

Retirement gave me the opportunity to purchase a farm in central PA and realize my life-long dream of living with horses. Another horsewoman entered my life,

Alvina Aucker. At the time she was in her teens, an Old Order Mennonite girl living on her family farm in Port Trevorton, PA (No photos please). Alvina, a gentle soul, wearing traditional long dress and white bonnet taught me to drive my Haflingers using my Meadowbrook cart, built by hand, by a local Mennonite gentleman.

The inspiration for writing *Lost Girl Missing* came from years of horse-keeping and caring for farm critters as well as having had the pleasure of raising a foal on the farm and going through the antics and growing pains of socializing, training, and watching her grow to a fine yearling!

Writing is a singular endeavor. But book production requires a small army. I couldn't have gotten this book into the hands of my readers without the following people. And so, I say many thanks to everyone for all that you have done. J. L. Saloff for pulling it all together page-by-page with her magic wand and fairy dust. Mark Saloff Designs for delivering an amazing cover, anticipating Fiona's journey. Ramona DeFelice Long for her editing advice and wisdom. My young and parent Beta readers for their honesty; Jamie and Kim Breyfogle, Heather and Owen McNabb, Betty McPherson, and Emma Paulette Specht. "In the beginning there were" ...my critique partners who honed my fledgling skills over many years and lifted me out of the Victorian Era.... I owe them more than I can say or write; Sheila Baranoski, Jim Breyfogle, Dave Freas (who always kicked my butt), Jen Welch, and Katie Yelinek

Obrigada one and all!